STELLA ALLAN

$\blacklozenge$

# A MORTAL AFFAIR

*Complete and Unabridged*

# ULVERSCROFT
*Leicester*

First published in Great Britain

First Large Print Edition
published 1999

Copyright © 1979 by Stella Allan

British Library CIP Data

Allan, Stella
  A mortal affair.—Large print ed.—
Ulverscroft large print series: mystery
1. Detective and mystery stories
2. Large type books
I. Title
823.9′14 [F]

ISBN 0–7089–4081–1

Published by
F. A. Thorpe (Publishing) Ltd.
Anstey, Leicestershire

Set by Words & Graphics Ltd.
Anstey, Leicestershire
Printed and bound in Great Britain by
T. J. International Ltd., Padstow, Cornwall

This book is printed on acid-free paper

Stella Allan began writing in 1970. *A Mortal Affair* is the fourth of her novels to be published and her second crime novel — a genre which she feels suits her.

She lives in Surrey and is married to retired army officer. During his period of service she lived in such assorted places as Malta, Inverness, Liverpool, Tripoli, Aberdeen and Singapore. The Allans have two grown-up daughters.

# A MORTAL AFFAIR

Frances Parry seemed to have it made. She was married to a Harley Street consultant, she had a beautiful home, wealthy friends — including the fascinating Bernard, her husband's friend since undergraduate days — and a creative job. But suddenly Frances's world was turned upside down; her home was sold, her sideline job became a vital means of livelihood, and Bernard, who had become her lover, was exposed as a criminal. And then Frances found that she herself was indulging in criminal activities in a deadly duel with the law.

*Books by Stella Allan*
*Published by The House of Ulverscroft:*

A DEAD GIVEAWAY
ARROW IN THE DARK

For Pat again
For all the same reasons
with love

# Acknowledgements

My thanks to my friends Chris Wilson-Smith and Brian Allen for their unstinted help on legal and professional matters, and to my brother, Peter Whitaker, who knows about guns.

# 1

Between the fish course and the meat Ellen said simply, 'I'm going to have a baby.' Her eyes, fastened on Duncan's face, saw him cast a swift, professional glance over her seated figure, automatically assessing the familiar symptoms of pregnancy, before he remembered he wasn't in his consulting-room and that she was more than just another of his patients. Watching the procession of his emotions, she read surprise, a detached concern, the vaguely concealed caution of not wanting to become involved again — once bitten twice shy — but as yet, no comprehension. To hasten it, she used a sledge-hammer. 'It's yours.'

He looked puzzled, bewildered, but not disbelieving, and for this she was grateful. She repeated calmly, 'I wouldn't lie to you, Duncan. It is yours.'

He said carefully, 'I don't understand. It's nearly six months since we — ' He broke off and fiddled with the cutlery on the table. He hadn't seen her since the final occasion on which they had gone to bed together and wrapped up the affair. It was all past history, an episode for which even now he could find no logical explanation, certainly no excuses. For a man in his profession it had constituted criminal folly. He had seen colleagues disgraced, fallen on a similar stony path, losing everything they had worked for in a promising career for the sake of an overwhelming physical attraction for a patient, and he had always considered them insane. It wasn't as if this had been something beyond their control, an all-engulfing passion, a mating of souls. It had begun as an expression of his pity and comfort and had terminated without recrimination or despair.

With her next words, all kinds of realizations started to seep through to practical consciousness. 'I'm over five months pregnant — just over,' she qualified, as if trying to make it sound less dire.

'Five months!' He couldn't conceal his shock. It should have come as no surprise — it figured. She must be that far gone if it were his, but five months was too late to do anything about it. Hard on his first reaction came a second jolt. He didn't know whether he was glad or sorry. It was his baby, his child, his son perhaps, who at any moment would be making movement, too far advanced to be sucked out and flushed down a convenient drain. Basely, her news brought a contigual feeling of self-justification and vindication, remembering the ten-year efforts of himself and Frances to produce a child during their marriage. All the messy, undignified tests to which they had both subjected themselves had proved negative, and though neither could be blamed for their continuing childlessness he, to a greater degree than Frances, had found the stigma of having been found wanting harder to bear. Now he had proof positive that it wasn't his fault. Not that he could ever divulge it to Frances, but he would know, and that went a long way towards healing his wounded pride.

All these impressions came tumbling in confusion through his mind which he made an attempt to clear for practicalities. He looked at Ellen, who sat waiting for him to speak. For the first time he noticed lines of strain in her pale, thin face. She had hardly any make-up on to disguise the indented blue shadows under the large grey eyes which were her main attraction.

Remembering his consulting technique, he smiled in an effort to relax her. 'You don't look very big.'

She shrugged. 'Thank goodness it's winter, and for the ethnic craze.' She looked down

3

at the layered mixture of clothes she was wearing — a full peasant skirt overlaid by a jumper and a smock, topped off by a fringed poncho. 'I shan't be able to hide it much longer.'

The waiter brought them veal and mushrooms in a white wine sauce and Duncan played for time, filling her glass from a bottle of Sauterne on the table. After they'd both taken a few mouthfuls of the food he said, 'Well, what are we going to do?'

She continued eating without speaking, not lifting her eyes from her plate, and when he looked across at her he could see two tears on either side of her nose course down and land on the chef's choice for the day. Duncan put his hand out and over the one that held her fork.

'Thanks for saying 'we'.' She laughed shakily.

'We're in this together,' he tried to reassure her, without the faintest idea of how he could smooth it all over. If it was a question of money, thank heavens he had enough to help with the kid and to keep the whole thing quiet. Adoption would probably be the best course. There were ways of arranging these matters discreetly. Ellen wouldn't want to make difficulties. Thank God she was the compliant, undemanding sort, not the type

4

to resort to blackmail or anything ugly like that. She was far too sweet. He felt warmly protective.

She took her hand from beneath his and fumbled in her sleeve for a handkerchief. Mopping up, she said apologetically, 'I'm sorry to be so silly, but that's so exactly what I hoped you'd say.'

'You didn't believe I'd let you down?'

She shook her head. 'Not really. But it was so long — I mean I hadn't intended to bother you again.' She looked decidedly more cheerful. She resumed eating. 'When will you do it, then?'

'Do what?'

She looked round and lowered her voice discreetly. 'The abortion. It'll have to be soon.'

With a chill he realized their wires were hopelessly crossed. 'At five months there can't be an abortion, Ellen. You've left it too late. If you wanted that you should have gone to someone sooner.' He could see that his attitude came as a complete surprise to her.

'I didn't know sooner. You know I've always been haywire. That's why Dr Inglis referred me to you in the first place, remember? When we parted everything stopped and started and stopped again. I didn't think anything about it. Just put it down to trauma. It's only this last fortnight I've been sure.'

'Well, I'm sorry. It wouldn't be safe, and even if it were, I couldn't possibly undertake a thing like that myself. You must see that.' He shook his head at the impossibility of the idea.

'Why not? You're a gynaecologist, aren't you? You do it for plenty of other people in that fancy clinic of yours, don't you?' There was a hardness in her voice that Duncan hadn't heard before.

He spread his hands. 'Of course I do, but I'm not personally involved with them. I've already committed the sin against the Holy Ghost as far as the General Medical Council is concerned in making love to you while you were my patient. What you need now isn't just a straightforward little vacuum job. It's a proper Caesar, dangerous and against the law. You wouldn't get a second opinion for a start. It's against all medical ethics.'

'It's a bit late to worry about ethics, isn't it?'

He had the grace to redden.

'All I know is you can do it, have done it for others. You've got the clinic, the staff. You don't need a second opinion. You're the boss.'

6

'You don't understand, there are forms and things. It would all come out.' He didn't know why he bothered to argue.

'You can fill in the forms. It'll all come out if you don't do it. I can't possibly have a baby, Duncan. You know I can't. You know my situation at home.' She beat her clenched fists on the table top. He thought of the bleak flat out at Palmers Green which she had described to him, her father crippled by arthritis, barely able to cope with his prematurely senile wife during the day while Ellen worked to provide for them all — the prison of their dependence upon her, the joyless prospect of their strong hearts outlasting their physical and mental capabilities. He knew it was out of the question. He simply hadn't thought it through.

'You could go away to have it, then offer it for adoption. I'll get your parents in somewhere — pay for them while you're off.'

'I'd lose my job. They'd only keep it for me if they knew I was having maternity leave, and I wouldn't be able to tell them that, would I? Adoption societies want to know about parents. You don't want that responsibility, do you?'

He put his head in his hands. 'It doesn't matter what I want. I only know I can't abort my own child.'

'Ah!' Ellen drew a long breath. 'That's it, isn't it? It's ego after all. You can't bring yourself to pull the chain on an extension of yourself.'

She was right, of course, yet it would be the most sensible, the neatest solution. It was as though she could see the cogs through which his mental processes were clicking, because after a silence she said in a much softer and more reasonable tone, 'Duncan, please think it over. I know you can arrange it so easily and it's what I have to do. The other way will break up my father to an even worse degree, louse up your good marriage — something I swear I never would want, and nor do you — ruin everything. I'd jump off the Post Office Tower but they need me at home.' It was a poor joke and he didn't smile. 'If you don't do it for me, I shall have to find someone who will, but they might not make such a good job of it and I know I'd be safe with you.' Her mouth tugged downwards at one corner in a wistful grimace of bravado that failed to camouflage her fear.

'All right. I'll think about it. I need a little time.' He meant he'd think about the whole ghastly mess, not about the possibility of performing the operation. That was definitely out in his own mind. There wasn't any harm in stalling her and letting her think

8

she was winning him round. That way she wouldn't do anything desperate until they spoke together again.

Something, some scheme must turn up. It always had before in his life when things had gone wrong. His parents, Bernard or Frances had seen to that. This time, of course, he couldn't rely on them or upon any outside agency, and the realization that this time he stood alone frightened him. The prospect was only marginally less fearful than that of disappointing and shaming his mother and father. Particularly his mother whose approbation, not easily won, he had sought during a lifetime of toeing her line.

★ ★ ★

Amelia Parry was a pretty woman whose fragile looks belied a cast-iron nature and resolve to push her husband up the tree of commerce and thence to the Civil Service, and Duncan into a suitably impressive profession of which she could boast. At thirty-six he could still rely on her to tell him when, in her opinion, he needed a haircut and she retained the power to make him feel suitably chastened if he failed to comply with the standards she set for her family and friends. Small wonder there had been an ever-increasing dropping-off of the latter, who inevitably found her impossible, proving to Amelia by their defection merely that they couldn't match Parry impeccability. Duncan had defied her once in his life, in his insistence on marrying Frances. He had learned a bitter lesson two years before when he had allowed Amelia to infiltrate and corrode a previous love-affair which had been terminated due to her poisonous offices and his own weakness, and he was determined not to lose Frances in the same fashion.

'She's not nearly good enough for you!' The familiar cry was raised as the tentacles of possession were flexed, but in the end Amelia Parry had been forced to back down, not without succeeding in making him feel overwhelmingly guilty for sticking to his guns. Resentful as he was of her domination, he had been unable to prise himself free of reliance on her partisan protection. The trappings of success, the Harley Street practice, the gracious Georgian house, the Bentley and the smart friends achieved to match his family's idea of a suitable lifestyle for an eminent consultant, helped to camouflage the stunted emotional growth of the man.

★ ★ ★

Today, driving home, it was typical that Duncan was far more worried about his parents' reaction to finding out about Ellen and the baby and his possible disgrace, than he was about his wife's.

His way took him past the point where it had all started, the bus stop where, in a moment of compassion, he had drawn up alongside the kerb and offered Ellen a lift to the tube station. It had been the end of April when she had been ushered into his office at the close of a routine day. It was raining heaven's hardest outside, and as his receptionist divested Ellen of the plastic mac and umbrella she had neglected to leave in the waiting-room, it was her very un-routine-ness that stirred his interest. Her wispy, bedraggled figure clad in chain store jumper and skirt was a far cry from the procession of well-groomed fashionably clad women who usually found their way to his consulting-rooms. Ellen looked more like one of his National Health Service clinic patients and he glanced down at her notes on his desk to check that a mistake had not been made. She resembled a pale, damp mouse, sitting opposite him, provoking within him a protective instinct which in the normal course of events he didn't find much opportunity to use. Frances needed no protection. He was painfully aware of the strength, sadly lacking in himself, with which his wife met the world. The clients who came to Harley Street had been educated not to show their vulnerability, however fearful they might be, and those at the hospital clinics were too numerous to be considered as individual personalities. Had Ellen been in either category, this whole thing would probably never have begun, but there she was, out of context sufficiently to stimulate a glimmer of interest, looking like a waif, speaking in pleasingly modulated tones, looking at him and answering his questions with a controlled, sweet gravity, and because she was the last case on his list he found himself taking the time to draw her out before examining her and pronouncing upon her condition.

'All's well,' he had said, turning from washing his hands, having given her time to put her clothes on. 'Nothing very alarming there. I'm going to give you a course of tablets that should do the trick.'

She had looked relieved. 'Dr Inglis mentioned the possibility of an operation.'

He smiled at her. 'No need for that. I'm sure this will respond to other treatment. There's nothing sinister there.'

'He thought there might be.' She was still

half afraid to believe him.

'Yes, well, there isn't. That's good news, isn't it?'

She'd been holding herself in tightly and now let out her breath on a sigh. 'Thank goodness.'

'You've been worried?'

'Yes, that's why I had to know the worst. Otherwise I wouldn't have — ' She'd been going to say she wouldn't have come privately and he made a mental note to get Mary to adjust the fee downwards at the appropriate time. 'Not so much for myself, but for Mother and Father. If anything happens to me I don't know how they'd manage. They're virtually helpless.' She stopped, aware that this was beyond the interest of a consultant. It had been later that the circumstances of her home life had been discussed between them and his realization of the barrenness of her life aroused an even stronger pity that took her to bed in an attempt to comfort. Her response had been passionately flattering, her temporary dependence upon him sweet, and he had felt altruistically that he was bringing a little warmth and tenderness to an arid scene. The ego boost was mutual, but being trained to self-deception, he didn't admit that to himself even now. If only the rain hadn't been bucketing down that night, if only he hadn't seen her at that benighted bus stop while he went to get his car. He could scarcely drive past enveloped in the upholstered comfort of the Bentley, ignoring her when she had come straight from his rooms.

The intended lift to the nearest tube station had extended itself to a drive all the way to Palmers Green which, in turn — God alone knew how — had developed into a further meeting, assignations, the whole works. It was incredible how easily such a thing could happen, started as curiosity, continued almost in spite of himself. The only calculated thing about the whole affair had been its ending, mutually, sensibly agreed, tidied up neatly. And now this!

He owed it to her to help her, but not to the possible detriment of his career. The idea of aborting the baby himself was repugnant. Even had the child been someone else's, ethically he was on dangerous ground, but his own son or daughter — it was impossible. He could hand her over to one of his colleagues, allow him to make the decision, but at five and a half months he knew what that decision would most likely be. She would have to have it, and having had it, part with it having seen it, held it. Once born, he knew he wouldn't be strong enough to resist seeing it too. His imagination fled down paths of fancy totally unconducive to solving the problem. Would it be dark like he had been, or fair like Ellen? If a boy, it would continue the line of Parrys, thus dissolving his mother's all too apparent disappointment and disapproval of his lack of provision of an heir to that name. He had to remind himself that his mother would not know — must not know.

The big car took the crest of Richmond Hill in its stride, the discreet purr of its engine unaltered by its extra exertion. At the top Duncan drew her to a halt to allow a man to use the pelican crossing. In the dipped headlights the pedestrian was recognizable as one of the inmates of the Star and Garter Home on his right. He wasn't a pretty sight. The mutilated face bore the massive scarring of burns worn for more than sixty years. The head was bald and what remained of his ears were a couple of crinkled frills round two black holes. One jacket sleeve hung empty while from the other protruded a metal stump complete with hook and clip. His progress across the road was negotiated by a series of unco-ordinated jerks and lunges which, once safely achieved, he turned and directed at Duncan the ghastly grimace that served as his travesty of a smile of acknowledgement. The car moved gently forward, the driver's dilemma peculiarly momentarily eased. The man's plight put his own problems into perspective. Nothing yet was so bad that he could not find some kind of a tolerable solution. Given the psychological moment, he might even make a clean breast of it to Frances. She had never failed him with her understanding. It was perverse therefore to feel often diminished by it, so that instead of seeking it as he yearned to do, he proved his manhood by telling himself he could manage without it.

# 2

Frances sang to herself as she reviewed the battle order for the dinner-party that she and Duncan were to give that evening. As she checked the cutlery in the place settings and centred the flowers more symmetrically between the silver candlesticks, she accompanied Sinatra being played on the radio with a neat improvisation of her own. She enjoyed entertaining, though tonight's affair would be stickier than most. What she had seen of the Crichtons and the Styles had not appealed to her, but it seemed they were important to Duncan. Latterly, cultivation of their ilk had taken precedence over long-term friendships of old colleagues he had left behind in the race for success. His mother called it 'knowing the right people' and applauded the new emphasis her son placed on its importance. Frances regretted it. She straightened a chair. Thank God for the leavening presences of Bernard and Liz. The table looked pretty set with appliquéd linen mats, delicate pink-bordered china and Waterford crystal. Satisfied, Frances came out of the dining-room, closing the door behind her.

The letter lying on the hall table again caught her eye, and she frowned as she had done when she had picked it up off the mat earlier in the day. It was addressed to Duncan in Amelia's hand, and Frances had lived with him long enough to know that he would never grow out of the uneasy apprehension that first sight of her weekly missive caused in him. She hoped, protectively, that today's contained no calculated disparagement.

Everything in Frances's own secure and happy background had encouraged her in an expectation of liking and being liked, so in the beginning it had been a puzzling disappointment to encounter the well-bred hostility with which Amelia Parry had reluctantly welcomed her into their clan. At the start of her marriage, Frances had sought to please, reasoning that his parents and she shared a unifying common cause in their love of Duncan. Subsequently, in the face of Amelia's unremitting possessive bitchiness, she had long since given up trying. She readily admitted that the defensively aggressive side of her character which she now offered to the older woman was equally as unattractive as Amelia's own, but it wasn't a relationship that could be mended.

18

Duncan's father was altogether different. Type-cast in the military mould from the days when officers had automatically been gentlemen, Alistair Parry's distinguished features wore the permanently anxious look of a man hag-ridden at home, who there opted for the line of least resistance. His professional success testified to qualities of determination, sound judgement and decisiveness, attributes Frances could only suppose he left at the office because there was no sign of them in his dealings with his wife. She remembered her first meeting with her father-in-law when Duncan had taken her, newly engaged, to Falconers and she had mistakenly at the time dismissed him as colourless. It had been slowly and later that they had established a comfortable rapport and Frances had discovered a depth of kindness and a soft core in Alistair that some might term weakness. Duncan had it too. Both he and his father had been attracted by strong women, but Frances hoped to God she bore no resemblance to Amelia! It was a sobering thought and one that pulled her up from time to time when she suspected she might be becoming too masterful. Recalling her impressions of that day long ago, the most vivid after Falconers itself, had been Amelia — but Amelia was so much a part of her surroundings that it was hard to imagine her away from the splendid background of the house and all the treasures in it. Falconers was not quite so splendid now. Frances had for some time noticed decorations that had been neglected and a diminution of some of the treasures. When she had mentioned this to Duncan, he had commented wryly that keeping the house going must constitute a perpetually increasing drain on Alistair's pocket and it went without saying that to live anywhere but Falconers would break Amelia's heart — if such an organ existed, Frances mentally added. If the wealth of Duncan's background and his parents had come as two surprises, Bernard had certainly been a third.

The noise of the garage door closing, followed by the sound of Duncan's key in the lock, prevented Frances's mind from slipping into a forbidden groove. Straightening the envelope on the table before he came through the front door, she went forward to greet him.

'You're nice and early.' She put her hands on his shoulders and gave him a proper kiss on the mouth. Their heads were level, his dark and stranded with grey, hers fair with naturally blonde streaks, and he noticed she'd had it recut and set so that it swung shortly about her face like a shining cap. Over her shoulder and through the glass doors into the dining-room he could see the polished regency table laid for the party, and inwardly his spirits sank.

'I forgot we'd got people coming tonight.' He couldn't quite keep the disappointment out of his voice.

'They're your friends, remember.'

'They're not that bad,' he demurred, moving towards the stairs on his way up to his dressing-room.

'They're phonies. So long as you don't mistake them for the genuine article. None of them would recognize a simple household gadget unless it was got up to look like a joke bag of golf-clubs or a champagne bottle in a bucket. That goes for people too. You don't think they'd give a tinker's cuss about you if you were in a jam, do you?'

She couldn't know how her words tightened his gut this particular evening. He tried to imagine going to Garfield Styles in his present predicament. He was a bluff, jovial type, a man of the world. He certainly wouldn't be shocked. It probably happened all the time in the circles in which he moved.

21

'Don't be so anti, Fran. It's inevitable that as one goes up one widens one's circle. Sometimes one has to do a little diplomatic cultivation. You do it beautifully.'

'If I do, it's for you — not them.' She blew him a kiss and watched him ascend the stairs. He went slowly, as if he were specially tired tonight, and her heart turned over with love for him as it always did when he was at his most vulnerable. She went into the dining-room and poured him a whisky, following him up to their bathroom where he stood, jacketless, inspecting his chin in the shaving mirror. While he took off his shirt and plugged in the razor Frances sat herself down on the lavatory lid to converse with him. Because he wasn't yet certain whether he could bring himself to tell her how his day had been, he forestalled her anticipated question by opening their conversation.

'Business good at the shop?'

'Building up. We had an order in bulk for Liz's new patchwork designs, cushions with curtains to match. It'll mean the hell of a lot of concentrated work but it's too good to pass up and may lead to others. This kind of thing snowballs.'

'So long as you and Liz don't bite off more than you can chew.' He dragged his top lip down to get at the stubble under his nose.

'We can always take on another hand if orders justify it. Eventually we'll be needing small factory premises. You'll see. I'll be able to clear all my bits and pieces out of the nursery.'

They had gone on calling it the nursery, the room next to their bedroom which had been set aside for that purpose when they had first moved into the house and which, as the years had passed without any sign of the child they both desired, had in turn served as a spare room to accommodate single visitors and then as a workroom for Frances and Liz before they had expanded into the shop. It was full of cotton, silk and velvet remnants, skeins of wool, graph paper and designs for their individual patchwork creations, cushions, bedspreads, tablecloths and curtains, and the ancient and modern tapestries for chair seats, stools and carpets that they dreamed up between them.

When Frances first met Liz Milne at a party, the latter was in the throes of picking up the pieces of her life after her husband had left her with a desk full of debts and five-year-old Kate. Liz was designing textiles freelance, but without much success, unable, because of having to look after the child, to give the job the full-time dedication so competitive a field demanded. The marriage break-up had been comparatively recent and her concentration and confidence were at low ebb. She had been thirty-three, five years older than Frances, and the two women had taken to each other immediately. Frances herself had a natural creative talent with colour and had always loved sewing and making soft furnishings, needlepoint pictures and the like, and Duncan had been tolerantly amused when later their common interest gave birth to the idea of going into business together. He had encouraged the scheme, if only because, occupied and enthusiastic, Frances had less time for brooding on their childlessness, and indeed, in the two years since they had embarked on their venture he had surprised less often the soft, sad longing in his wife's eyes when discussion centred round the young families of friends. Kate was partially responsible. Frances clearly loved her and was constantly admonished by Liz for spoiling her.

She was an intelligent child with straight black hair and a square fringe, with a precocious sensitivity towards her mother born of the shock of waking one morning to find the daddy they both adored didn't adore them. Frances spent a lot of time in the small flat over the shop that had been adapted and decorated as Liz and Kate's new home, and Kate came and spent days or nights happily at the house on Richmond Hill, when Liz was going out somewhere or she was working on a design that had to be rushed through and required all the floor and table space at the flat. Liz seldom visited on her own. She didn't feel altogether comfortable with Duncan, although he behaved in a friendly enough fashion towards her, but in his presence she felt her sense of failure more acutely. She hoped it wasn't envy on her part because he and Frances had such a beautiful home and so deeply founded a security in their own relationship. Perversely too, in their house, she felt guilty for having Kate, which never happened when it was just the three of them in her own place. Hill House seemed a perfect stage set, built for players who had not materialized upon the scene.

Duncan switched off the razor and splashed after-shave over his face. His cheeks were full and pink, making him look younger than his age. His shoulders were square and muscled under the harsh bathroom light but there was no disguising the incipient slackening of the stomach, once flat and hard, which the belt of his trousers dented. For all that, he was still handsome. Frances put out her hand and laid it against his hairless chest.

'I love you,' she said.

He concentrated on the mirror. Would she still love him if she knew? Could he risk her disfavour — her forgiveness? She didn't notice his silence but skipped to her next theme.

'Dolly came round just after I got back from the shop.' Frances grimaced. 'She had to make do with a cup of tea in the kitchen while I got on with the meal.'

'I suppose she wanted to know why she hadn't been invited.' Dolly was a cross they both had to bear, but mostly Frances.

'I won't stop, Frances, I can see you're entertaining some of your important friends.' Frances sarcastically imitated her sister's clipped, complaining whine. 'Of course it's nice to be able to afford to have people in. It makes a difference when you can go out and buy what you want. I'd like to ask you and Duncan more often to my humble abode but I'm sure he's not used to cauliflower cheese, and most people can't run to a stock of liqueurs.' Frances sighed.

'Don't let her bug you, baby.' He said it out of the side of his mouth in a Bronx accent.

26

'I always do. It's not as if she's hard up. She's got her share of Father's money and a good salary.'

'She's been jealous of you all your life — your mother first and now you. She's not going to change at fifty.'

Frances got off her perch and started running the bath. 'She was prettier than me, she had all the marriage prospects in the world, but no one was good enough. It's her fault she never got a man. I try to do everything I can for her but she always makes me feel I'm playing Lady Bountiful. You aren't listening.'

He'd wandered away into his dressing-room and returned without his clothes to feel the bath water with his big toe before climbing in and settling down under the foam made by the bath oil Frances had added.

'I've heard it all before,' he said. 'Spite, envy, malice and all uncharitableness.' By God, Dolly would have a field day with Frances if he were disgraced. A rift in their lute, an illegitimate child and himself struck off would be her idea of a salutary lesson in life for her fortunate sister. He sighed and shut his eyes. Frances, looking at him, felt an unaccountable chill.

'Is anything wrong?'

27

'No. Just weary.' He kept his lids closed. There was a silence which he was on the verge of breaking with the unburdening of his spirit. He took a breath and opened his eyes, but Frances had gone to change and the moment passed.

★ ★ ★

When he came downstairs, Duncan saw a letter on the hall table that he must have overlooked when he came in. He skimmed through two opening paragraphs before he reached the hard matter.

Some rather wonderful news has just come through and naturally your father and I want you to be the first to know that he is definitely to receive his 'K' in the New Year's Honours. I know you will be as proud of him and delighted as I am and that you will be writing to tell him so. [Out of habit she reminded him of his duty and his manners. Duncan stifled prickings of resentment.] He has worked so hard and selflessly all these years and it is gratifying that the Powers that Be have recognized his efforts and obviously appreciate them. We knew that his name had been put forward but I said nothing in case of a disappointment, but confirmation of the honour came today, so you will soon be able to own us as Sir Alistair and Lady Parry. How does that sound to you?

To Duncan, re-reading and digesting the tone of the missive it sounded like another nail being hammered into his coffin. The chasm between his father's knighthood and his own dishonour widened the differences between them, making his situation less possible to communicate to anyone. He had all the more to live up to now, and his sense of inadequacy deepened.

Frances, coming downstairs looking pretty and sophisticated in cherry-red crêpe that clung and then fluted into fluid lines, caught his expression.

'Bad news?' she asked, turning to give him her back view so that he could adjust her zipper.

'On the contrary.' Duncan contrived a smile and gave her the letter while he attended to doing her up.

Frances read it. 'Well, isn't that splendid. She'll be very happy!' Being human, she was unable totally to eliminate sarcasm. He was silent. 'I'm really glad for your father.' She turned, pulling his arms around her waist and placing her hands against his chest. 'I'm sorry. I'm getting like Dolly. Don't be cross with me.'

'I'm not cross.'

'What then?' She scrutinized him closely. 'You're something — but I don't quite know what. Worried? Depressed perhaps? This hasn't got you down?' She waved the letter in her hand.

'Good heavens no. Why should it? I'm very pleased, and proud for them.' He made himself look straight into her eyes. He saw them soften.

'And I'm very proud of you. I love you.' She kissed him. 'I love you very much.'

'I know,' he said maddeningly. It was their ritual.

'Mm!' She closed her eyes and held her scented cheek against his. 'We're so lucky. It's so good — what we've got.' The ache inside him to cast himself upon her mercy made him tighten his grip on her. 'All the letters in the alphabet after your name wouldn't make you any more precious to me. I love you for what you are.'

He held her to him, looking beyond her blankly, only certain that he couldn't risk losing her trust.

★ ★ ★

Three double gins before dinner, Frances's expertly prepared Salmon Mornay and its attendant carefully chosen wines, did nothing to lift Duncan's increasing depression. In the effort not to appear abstracted to his guests, he downed more alcohol than he was used to, but instead of serving as a temporary anaesthetic, it had the effect of making him see things with a profounder, dismal clarity and stripping from his companions their sophisticated intellectual aura, revealing the shallow depth of the superficial relationship that he had been pleased to call friendship. Frances was right. He and she had nothing in common with these people. Listening to Marcia Styles, plump and petitely pretty, with tiny fluttering hands and a high affected voice which was now questioning Frances about the shop, Duncan heard her say in a bemused tone:

'And you *sell* them? But my dear Frances what made you want to start on this sort of thing? I mean — ' she batted her eyelashes around the room to indicate the comfortable luxury with which they were surrounded — 'it's not as if you *have* to work, is it?' The question was purely rhetorical. The notion that Frances's hard-earned profits from the shop should form an essential part of the income of people in their category was too ridiculous. What would her reaction be to his losing his job, his fall from grace? A sexual misdemeanour too! So much more unsavoury and reprehensible than the decidedly questionable transactions of which Sir Miles Crichton had been bragging throughout the meal. He had earned his knighthood skating on thin ice and the smell of some of the deals he had instigated might have accounted for the sneering tilt of her ladyship's long nose. In Duncan's shoes, Sir Miles wouldn't have balked on a matter of principle. Duncan could assess what his attitude would be.

'Are you bloody insane, old chap? You're in the ideal position to hush it all up. Your own nursing home! Enough said. Discreet operation — not even against her will, what? You've done it before — you will again. Question of ethics? Splitting hairs, old boy. It's a fine point — too fine for me. Don't want to upset the little woman, do you? She's not like Joan. We agree to go our own ways. I can see it's not like that with you, what?'

He'd be right. Duncan sighed. But then the Crichtons were blessed with a daughter and a son of their own and were untrammelled by conscience or the Hippocratic oath. He looked up and caught Bernard's eyes. The smile in them was reassuring and reminded him of the solidity of their friendship — tried and trusted. Bernard had bailed him out once before. He would help him now. Perhaps he could get him alone before the evening was over.

# 3

Frances, smiling prettily and responding to Miles Crichton's blandishments with as much courtesy as she could muster, mentally calculated how long it would be before they would all go home. The meal had been a success and her guests appeared to be enjoying themselves, but even before the evening had commenced a pall had descended upon her spirits which had nothing to do with her antipathy to the Crichtons and the Styles. In the event, they had proved inoffensive and flatteringly appreciative and could not be held accountable for her vague disquiet. Depression was too strong a word, but in attempting to analyse its source, she realized it stemmed from Duncan. His manner had been off-key since his homecoming. Frances, who was familiar with all the nuances, had a premonition of an anxiety withheld, a withdrawal into partial isolation. Worries about his work were usually expressed volubly in an outpouring of frustration against the idiocies of bureaucracy or soul-searching into reasons why something had gone wrong. However much he was the self-assured professional to his colleagues and patients, Duncan's confidence had always needed her as a sounding-board at home, to encourage, approve and support. Watching him now engaged in some socially flirtatious banter with Liz, who was looking very striking tonight in a dress of golds and browns to match her spectacular hair and eyes, Frances asked herself whether she was imagining things — acting like a mother hen, over-protective, over-maternal. That was the trouble, having no babies. One's natural instincts demanded a channel and the love she would have given a child spilled over into what she felt about her husband.

Passion had died years ago when she had realized he did not require it of her. It had been present during their brief engagement and the first months of their marriage, before the recognition that her spontaneity not only embarrassed him but aroused his suspicions. In fact she had been a virgin when they married. When she laughingly admitted it had been touch and go — more touch than go, he had registered distaste at the crudity. Even before he had told her about what had happened at Cambridge, she suspected she was the first woman he had possessed, though after University and his years as a medical student, common sense had insisted that this was highly unlikely. It was hard to credit a youth mis-spent with Bernard as mentor would have been conducive to virginity. There had been an occasion long ago, shortly after her marriage, when Bernard had made a pass at her after a party they had all three attended, and at the conclusion of which Duncan had retired to bed with a delicate stomach. When she cared to, Frances remembered pleasurably the sensations evoked by Bernard's practised, marauding hands, in delicious contrast to Duncan's comfort-seeking mouth at her breast. At the time she had eminently sensibly made light of them both being over-full of champagne, and the episode had never been referred to again or repeated. Her doubt that he would even remember was belied by the way he sometimes looked at her, and she didn't altogether trust him — or herself. Duncan's total fascination with his friend was another contributory cause of her wariness in dealing with Bernard.

★ ★ ★

The two men had met as new boys at Harrow and had continued friends through the school and afterwards at Cambridge, where they had shared rooms. Bernard's parents lived abroad.

36

His father had been a medical missionary in Sarawak, Borneo and Indonesia, for the most part in isolated regions unsuitable for healthy fun holidays for a schoolboy, so Bernard spent the majority of his vacations at Falconers with Duncan and Amelia and Alistair Parry. His mother had died during an outbreak of cholera during Bernard's last year at school. She had been buried near the Mission that now became his father's sole reason for continuing his own life. The bond between father and son, tenuously kept intact by his mother's letters, without them slackened and finally dissolved. Even then Bernard had a way with women. He buttered Amelia up shamelessly with his own brand of cheeky, flattering gallantry which she adored but would have allowed from no one else. To him she yielded an affection unfettered by the maternal responsibility to make him into a credit to her.

'Weren't you ever jealous of him?' Frances once asked Duncan.

'Of Bernard? Good heavens no. I was only too relieved they approved of someone I liked.'

It hurt Frances to think of the boy Duncan basking in such vicarious approbation.

'Besides, you chose me, not him. I'll never know why.' He had forgotten that the choice had been made before Frances had seen Bernard.

He was taller than Duncan with the lean, wiry build that didn't run to fat in later years. His face was long and angular with skin stretched tautly over the cheekbones and hollowing down to where his jaw jutted sharply and squarely. He was pale, in contrast to his black hair and brows which rose above eyes that looked out on the world with the amused cynicism that also twisted his mouth. He possessed a biting wit, tinged with enough malice to make one ashamed for laughing at it. Religion was its favourite butt and this, Frances suspected, had much to do with his parents' calling. Their Christian charity had not begun at home as far as Bernard was concerned, and resentment of this fact occasionally showed through chinks in the armour of his self-sufficiency. He dressed impeccably in expensive taste — navy pin-striped three piece suits, Gucci shoes, gold half-hunter and chain, gold cufflinks and a diamond-headed tiepin. His casual clothes were elegant and beautiful and he had a flat in Brandon Court off Belgrave Square full of carefully chosen antiques, valuable pictures and a priceless collection of flintlocks and old pistols. It all added up to a combination of personality, affluence and style which was well nigh irresistible and powerfully attractive. Frances, aware of it and susceptible as any other woman, nevertheless found herself intermittently chilled by glimpses of a fundamental lack of warmth in Bernard, a cold calculation revealed only transiently, which she found unaccountably disturbing. Soon after their marriage she had opined as much to Duncan. He had been genuinely astonished.

'Cold? Old Bernard? That shows how little you know about him, darling. He's been more than a friend to me.' His face wore the familiar look of hero-worship to which Frances was already accustomed when the subject of Bernard cropped up. Irritated by it, she said lightly, 'Oh, I know as far as you're concerned the sun shines out of his arse, but there's something about him — I can't quite put my finger on it.' She had been sitting at the dressing-table, brushing her hair before getting into bed and he had come up behind her and laid his hands on her shoulders.

'You mustn't be jealous of him, Fran.'

She sat still under his grasp, her eyes questioning his in the mirror.

'Mustn't I?' she asked quietly.

His expression was shocked. 'Good God no. What are you thinking? There's nothing like that. Heavens, that's the last thing.' He stood silent, as though his train of thought had taken him beyond her momentarily.

'What is it?'

Recalling the present, he sat down beside her, taking her hand in his. 'There's something I want to tell you — have wanted to tell you — but now your saying that makes me wonder if you'll understand.'

'Does it concern Bernard?'

'Yes. But I don't want you to think that I — '

'If it's something that happened before I met you I don't think I want to hear.' She had a premonition she wasn't going to like any of it, but having come this far, he seemed hell bent on going ahead.

'I want you to understand what sort of a person he is, but you must promise never to mention it.'

'Promise.' To lighten the tension she wet her finger and drew it across her throat, but he didn't smile.

'There was a young man at Cambridge — during my last year before our finals. He and I had some kind of a thing going.' He glanced at her to see how she was taking it. He could see that she immediately understood but she asked, 'What sort of a thing?' to make sure. When he didn't reply she said gently, 'You were lovers?'

Duncan looked uncomfortable. 'That's an extravagant word to describe a callow infatuation on the boy's part.'

'There's no need to split hairs with me.'

Duncan cleared his throat and she could see he was deeply moved by a painful memory. 'Bernard and I were both leaving Cambridge shortly for good. The affair was over. I explained as best as I could to this chap that it was over, that we couldn't expect to meet after he and I had come down. I was just starting in medicine. Rumours of that sort of thing could be damaging to my career. The boy had become too possessive. He could have made trouble. He *did* make an ugly scene.' Duncan turned away to look out of the window. Frances noticed the knuckles of his hands hanging loosely at his sides were quite white. 'He put himself on the railway line. A train cut off his head and legs. He left a note. There was one initial on the envelope, the message inside was not addressed. The initial was 'P'. He'd always called me by my surname — Parry.' He stopped, then said irrelevantly, 'His name was David.' The silence hung between them. 'I was terrified of the disgrace, but mostly of my mother.' He laughed without humour. 'Ironically, it was always the wrong sort of girls she was

41

warning me about. What it would do to her — and Father. By hellish bad luck David's father was some big noise in one of the old man's subsidiary companies. He could have crucified him in commerce. You can see what a hell of a stink it would have raised for everyone. As it was, the scandal was bad enough, but not as bad as it might have been.'

'As it was?'

He looked at her closely for the first time. 'That's where Bernard came in. He took the blame. He was with me when I found the note. He changed the 'P' to a 'B'. There was nothing to prove David hadn't written it to him. No one else knew about our relationship. We'd been discreet, always meeting in my rooms, mine and Bernard's that is. It could have been either of us. Bernard was sent down. He went to Falconers and eventually took his law finals independently.'

The room was quiet while Frances grappled with a number of conjectures, all of them unpleasant. In her superficial knowledge of Bernard's character, the nobility of his behaviour seemed inconceivable. She finally said, 'But why? Why should he do it? What was in it for him?'

'Nothing but friendship, Fran. And

gratitude. Falconers had been the only home he had known. He said he had nothing to lose, whereas my father and I had everything. That's why I had to tell you the sort of person he is.'

'Greater love hath no man! Did your parents ever know?'

'About me? Jesus, no. It would kill them. Certainly kill me stone dead with them. They were very sympathetic to Bernard, though. When it's not their own kids parents can afford to take a broad view.' It was said without trace of cynicism. 'The old man did all he could to help.'

'He might have welcomed that chance to help you.'

Duncan shivered. 'He might, but I couldn't risk it. I suppose you're wondering how I could have let Bernard do it but I was completely shot away at the time. David's death was a ghastly shock. Bernard eventually made me see I wasn't to blame — the boy was unbalanced. It could have happened to anybody. Unluckily it was me.'

Something in her face stopped him. 'You don't think I'm a raving queer, do you Fran? I wouldn't have told you about this episode if that were true. It was the only time. An experimental stage.'

'I understand,' she said quietly. She could

read the relief in his eyes. She wasn't lying. It was realistic to accept the fact that most men reached maturity with a homosexual experience behind them. That didn't frighten her. More disconcerting was the degree of self-delusion and the ready shovelling off of responsibility or guilt. Unwilling to be disillusioned herself, Frances relegated such unwelcome sentiments and determined to be strong for them both.

In the ten intervening years Frances had kept her promise. The Cambridge episode was dead and buried, like the unknown David. Inevitably Bernard's role in it had coloured her estimation of him, and her knowledge of that encouraged her to look beneath the façade of his flippant sophistication for the qualities of loyalty and dependability which, she reasoned, must exist. She was forced to admit she must have been wrong about him. She had, after all, been wrong about Duncan. Altogether, she had not been the best judge of character.

At least Bernard's sacrifice had ultimately had no detrimental effect upon his career. Both men had come a long way, Frances thought, watching them now at table — successful and respected, the eminent gynaecologist and the reputed lawyer with their fashionable practices. In her *naïveté*

Frances hadn't supposed that solicitors made all that much of a killing, but indubitably Bernard must. Increasingly over the past few years there had been evidence of a spreadingly lavish lifestyle — faster cars, more expensive holidays and an expansion of his artistic acquisitions. She knew that he played the stock market and had made a number of coups, and being single he hadn't the same financial responsibilities as Duncan. All the same, for a man who had started without Duncan's advantages, he had come on apace.

★ ★ ★

The party was finally over. When Duncan returned from speeding the final guest, Frances was already at the sink, stacking the dishes and putting the remains of the food in the fridge. They had a shared system for the clearance of the debris and soon everything was washed and put away. Duncan was morosely silent throughout the operation and Frances experienced a renewed stab of the premonition that something was wrong.

'It went better than I expected.' She was taking off her apron and turning out the lights.

'The meal was delicious. You did them proud.'

'So did you. I know it was an effort. You could have done without them tonight. You were tired.'

'Did it show?'

'Only to me.' She hoped to have given him an opening but he responded by starting up the stairs, leaving her to follow. Better not to press it tonight, she thought. Sooner or later he would confide in her.

★ ★ ★

Sooner or later she'd have to know, thought Duncan, lying awake in the dark beside her. He had no guard against her. She loved him enough to be aware of all his moods. No one else had ever cared so much — except Bernard. He needed her to go on caring. Sooner or later. If he were to do what Ellen wanted, it would have to be sooner. Sooner the better. It was the only sensible way out and it was what she wanted. Why should he be such a fool to deny her when it answered his own problems? Duncan twisted uneasily on his dilemma until he slipped into a fitful dream-laden doze. When he awoke he had decided that he could afford neither conscience nor sentiment.

# 4

Ellen sat on the white honeycombed nursing home bedspread and wondered whether she was meant to be getting undressed and into bed. No one had told her when she had signed in and been ushered into her room, but everyone had been very kind, smiling and welcoming. This had been a relief. She had half expected to be treated like the pariah she felt. In the permissive society it was evident that it was only she who stigmatized herself. She hadn't been prepared for how bad it felt. Up till now she had been too desperate to prevent its birth to think of the baby as a person. She had needed to be so single-minded in her persuasion of Duncan to perform the operation that perversely it was now, with her object achieved, that she wondered and regretted and vaguely imagined how things could have been arranged otherwise. As someone with a fear of flying forgets the terror of being airborne on the moment of landing, she forced herself to remember the desperation and panic that had brought her to this moment. She had no option but to go through with it, wished none, but it would have been easier if the child had not so recently moved inside her. She had woken three nights previously to feel its pulsing throb, like a palpitation low in her stomach, and had been surprised until she had realized what was happening. If only it could have waited another three days. Ellen put her hands against her body under her smock, fearing to feel further evidence of the baby's independent life force.

The ground-floor room was restfully painted in pale eau-de-nil and the cushions of an easy chair matched the walls. There was a built-in cupboard, a dressing-table with a hand-worked runner on it and a washbasin and mirror built into an arch facing the bed. Through the window there was a pleasant view of grass and two rose-beds. Ellen had never been in hospital herself but Burtoncroft was certainly a far cry from the noisy, battered outpatients' wards where she wheeled her father for treatment when his arthritis tightened its clamplike hold. She had Duncan to thank for her comparative luxury. Otherwise God knows where she might have been. It didn't occur to her to think that she also had him to thank for her present troubles. For that she shared responsibility with him. She wondered when he would come to see her. He had said he would drop in during the afternoon, and of course he would be with her when they put her under tomorrow. He had promised that. She hadn't had any time to herself to think during the past week. There had been so much to see to. Fortuitously, she had a fortnight's holiday owing to her, and although Mr Marshall had not been pleased when she had announced her intention of taking it with so little notice, he had soon relented when he heard it had been questionable whether she could get her parents settled and that the Social Welfare people had unexpectedly come up with two vacancies for them in a Council home to coincide with her arrangements. Mr Marshall knew Ellen's background and considered she had a thin time at home. Besides, she was normally conscientious and a reliable worker.

Her mother had presented no problems, having reached that docile stage of senility that required for the most part the shovelling in of food at one end and the cleaning and drying of the other to keep her contented. So long as her husband accompanied her she had had little grasp of the temporary move. Mr Birch, on the other hand, had had to be cajoled, coerced and jollied along to accept the scheme, and right up until this very

49

morning Ellen had feared he might put his cantankerous foot down. Here, surrounded by peace and silence, Ellen had too many hours ahead for introspection, and she feared them and her inactivity which encouraged doubts.

She got off the bed and started to undress, folding her clothes neatly and putting them away in the cupboard. In the glass she looked sideways at her thickening body. To anyone who hadn't known it before, it didn't look particularly pregnant. She fantasized the baby away and wondered what she was doing in this place.

There were footsteps outside the door. Ellen hurriedly pulled her blue cotton nightie down to hide her nakedness. There was a knock at the door and a man came into the room and introduced himself as the anaesthetist. He smiled at her too as he took her blood pressure and pulse, looked at her arms for veins and sounded her chest. After he'd gone, Ellen lay back in bed and waited for Duncan.

He came at five-thirty. By then she'd had tea and been shaved. The sister came in with him and he was very professional as he smiled at her and said, 'Hullo, Miss Birch. Everything all right?' — and as she nodded, 'Good. Well, let's have a look at you, shall we?' He drew up her nightie and felt her tummy, listened to the child's heartbeat a moment, not looking at her. Ellen wished he didn't have to see her like that, lying there like a plucked chicken. It was obscene for her lover to see her that way, but of course he was no longer her lover, merely a mechanic poring over the intricate mechanism of another engine. A nurse came in and spoke to the sister, who left the room with a murmured apology, closing the door behind her, leaving them alone. Duncan tucked the bedclothes around her.

'How are you?' His voice had altered and she was able to reach for his hand and hold it for courage.

'A bit frightened.'

'I know. It'll be all right tomorrow. I promise you.'

She nodded. 'I trust you. I'm glad you're doing it.' She hesitated. 'Is it very awful for you?'

His face tightened. 'I shan't think about myself, don't worry on that score. I've taken a decision. I shan't mess it up. You're the patient, you're my sole concern.'

'Thank you.'

The sister returned. Duncan stood up. 'I'll see you tomorrow then. You're first on my list.'

She gave a tiny wave and he raised his hand in a reciprocal salute.

'Make sure she gets a good night's sleep, sister,' he instructed as they went out of the room together.

★ ★ ★

They gave Ellen two tablets to take with some Ovaltine after a light supper. She wasn't used to sleeping pills and they knocked her out cold until the next morning. She was still heavy-eyed when someone shot a needle into her arm and told her to count up to ten in the ante-room beside the theatre. Duncan had leaned over her with some reassuring words and was holding her hand when her voice trailed away on 'three'.

He had been afraid of his emotions dominating his brain, of being hesitant when the moment arrived, of not being capable of seeing the beastly business through, in spite of his confident words to Ellen the previous evening, but he needn't have feared. When it came to the crunch, his training and professionalism carried him through the first incision and into the womb. At the appropriate time, he lifted out the foetus of his son from the gash in the exposed square of white flesh before him, and handed it without a tremor to a nurse standing beside him with a receptacle, waiting for it. She moved away and Duncan turned his head back to his patient. He didn't want to see what the nurse did with it. He absorbed himself in the ritual of swabbing and stitching and removing clamps and when, at the end, he had finished, he was conscious of a job well done. It had seemed such an insurmountable hurdle and it had gone off like any routine operation, better than many. He didn't feel any of the things he had expected — no guilt, no sorrow, no fear, no remorse. He felt quite numb and astonishingly tired.

The fatigue he shook off with a cup of Matron's strong coffee and two cigarettes, while Ellen was wheeled back to her room and he prepared to be immersed in the rest of the morning's list. It was late lunch-time before Duncan could make a moment to see her, and when he did, the nurse by her bedside told him she had come round briefly before lapsing back again into a deep sleep. They had removed her theatre cap and her hair was spread on the pillow around her face which was faintly flushed in slumber.

'Everything satisfactory?' he asked the nurse.

'Yes, sir.'

'Good. I'm going home for a bite of lunch,

then I have to see two patients. I'll look in again at tea-time.'

★ ★ ★

Frances's Mini was in the garage when Duncan arrived at Hill House. He had forgotten that she had said she would be working at home on some new designs this afternoon, and he wished he had stayed and snatched a sandwich in the anonymity of a bar in town. He needed time to collect himself after the strain, not so much of the morning, but of the tension leading up to it, and he didn't feel ready to face someone who knew him as well as Frances did. It was too late to reverse down the drive. Entering the scullery from the garage door, he heard voices in the kitchen and he was instantly relieved that the presence of a third party would spare him an immediate tête-à-tête with his wife, even though that third party turned out to be Dolly, who normally irritated him unendurably. As he came upon them, his sister-in-law, who stood draped in what she considered was an elegant pose in the doorway, moved aside to let him pass and treated him to a languid smile of greeting.

Dolly Moodie never just stood anywhere.

She arranged herself in a series of studied movements, imitating actresses she had admired in the nineteen-forties. She had been a very pretty girl, and so many people had told her so that she had wasted most of her life searching for somebody suitably worthy upon whom to bestow her charms, ignoring in the quest any number of eligibles who had wanted to marry her and who, for one reason or another, she deemed not quite suitable. She was twenty years older than Frances and had fallen between so many stools looking for the perfect man, that now, at fifty, her disappointment in discovering that no such animal existed was camouflaged by scorn for those of her sex who had happily settled for flesh and blood men instead of idols. She liked to patronize Frances in private and in front of strangers, although she couldn't get away with it so well if Duncan were present. To him she deferred in business matters, questions of investments, and discussions of the stock market. Dolly had worked in a bank since she was eighteen and would, God willing, until she was sixty-five, so she considered she had the edge on Frances in financial matters. Emotionally, her dependence upon Frances was total. She had lived with their parents until they had both died suddenly within a year of each other, and although under the terms of their wills Dolly had inherited a comfortable house and its valuable contents, she had sold everything up in a panic, accepting the first inconsiderable offer, and had moved herself into a flat on Frances's doorstep where she had been the bane of her sister's life ever since. She sulked ostentatiously if she felt she had been excluded from an expedition, drew attention to her pitiful solitary existence if she knew there were to be guests at Hill House, and deplored the fact that she had to stand at draughty bus stops while others more fortunate had cars. She had a sapping effect on Frances's generous, open nature, like a great white leech. Because of her consciousness of her own good fortune, Frances could never quite bring herself to tell Dolly to go to hell. Typically, it was Frances who was cutting sandwiches and making coffee while Dolly stood in the way, a sherry glass in her hand.

'Hullo, girls.' Duncan forced himself to brightness. He never used a natural tone in Dolly's presence so Frances was not alerted by his voice. As she raised her face sideways for his kiss, she glanced at him, detecting a tautness about his eyes.

'I wasn't expecting you. I thought it was your rush day.'

'It is. I just felt like a break. Can I join you?' He hooked out a stool with his foot and sat down on it. 'No work today, Dolly?'

'It's my lunch-hour. I came in to give Fran my library books but she's just told me she went to the library yesterday. I wish I had known. I'll have to wait until next week now. I shan't have anything to read.'

'Why don't you take them down yourself?' Duncan helped himself to a sandwich and bit into it.

'I would, but it means lugging them to the bank and then rushing along at closing time, then the others have got to be carried back. They're heavy when you haven't got transport. You wouldn't realize.' She forced a martyred little laugh.

'Why don't you get yourself a car and learn to drive?' Duncan went on munching.

'Oh, I don't think I'm temperamentally suited to driving — not like Fran. I'm too nervous and sensitive. Besides — ' she halted herself in time. When you've already got a cow, why buy milk?

Frances wiped down the Formica top, clearing the bread crusts into the bin, and brought the coffee to the table. Dolly subsided on to a stool and was offered a sandwich. Before she took it she picked up her plate and inspected it through her bifocals, then wiped it with the paper napkin Frances had provided. It was pure habit but it was a ritual that made Duncan grit his teeth, particularly in restaurants where cutlery and glasses were all polished by Dolly before use. That she might 'catch something' was one of her phobias. It was one that gave rise to a certain amount of coarse comment from Duncan. 'No wonder she's still a virgin if everything's got to be disinfected before use!' He shot a glance at Frances who pressed her leg against his under the table in acknowledgement of their private joke. It was suddenly immensely good to feel her so close, so in tune. It was what he badly needed. She was so right for him, so fine, and he'd been such a damned fool, playing with fire, perilously close to endangering both their happiness. Well, that was over. He'd taken the consequences and done what he had to do. He'd got a new chance and he'd learned a painful lesson; nothing came free and the cost had been dear but it had been paid. He put his hand on Frances's leg, feeling its comforting warmth through her jeans. The telephone rang in the hall.

'I'll go. It'll be for me.' Duncan stood up and gulped down the coffee remaining in his cup. 'No peace for the wicked.' He lifted the receiver. 'Parry here.'

He heard Matron start to speak. 'Mr Parry, thank heavens I've caught you. Yes, an emergency, I'm afraid. Miss Birch — '

He didn't wait for much more.

'I'm on my way.' Dropping the receiver, he turned and found Frances behind him. She saw his face and said, 'What is it?'

'Someone's dying,' he told her. He looked ghastly, ashen pale with grey shadows in the hollows of his cheeks as he moved towards the door. Frances opened it and ran with him to the car. She squeezed his arm as he got in.

'Good luck, darling.' She slammed the door. 'Good luck!' Her cry followed him. He was going to need plenty of luck all right, but if what Matron had said was true, it was a commodity fast running out for him.

# 5

Ellen died five minutes after he reached her. There was nothing he could do except to make futile and ineffectual attempts to stem the massive haemorrhage as her life ebbed out under his hands and her shallow breath expired on a last faint sigh. By the time he made the nursing home they had her rigged up for transfusion, but the incoming blood couldn't compensate for the body's substantial loss, and unbelievably swiftly she was gone.

'I don't understand it. She was perfectly all right.' Duncan knew he was repeating himself but he couldn't think of anything else to say. Less than an hour ago he had seen her lying pinkly warm in sleep. Now the yellow waxen mask of death already covered her features. He remembered his promise to her only yesterday. 'It'll be all right. I shan't mess it up.' But he had.

'I trust you,' she had said. 'I trust you.'

He put his hands over his eyes but he couldn't blot out the memory of her unquestioning faith in him as she had spoken. Matron had her hand on his arm.

'I've sent for some tea, Mr Parry. Come along into my office.' He went with her, trying to control an overwhelming desire to cry. The last time he had cried had been when David had died. He had been afraid then too. He cleared his throat and got a grip on himself.

'What happened?' He must have sounded condemnatory because Matron's first words were defensive.

'There was no negligence, Mr Parry. Miss Birch came round partially once, before you saw her while the nurse was sitting with her. She came round more fully a short while later and spoke to nurse. She was quite conscious then. Nurse made her comfortable, then left her for quarter of an hour. When she returned Miss Birch complained of sudden pain. Almost immediately there was the onset of haemorrhage, the patient went into shock. I called you.' Matron spread her hands. 'You know yourself. It can be like that. Luckily it seldom happens, but there is always some risk. The operation was completely successful. No blame can in any way be attached to you, Mr Parry.'

He was silent, and she continued, no doubt meaning to ease the misplaced sense of guilt she imagined he was feeling. 'There was an inherent risk in this case, the pregnancy being so far advanced, but there were no doubt sound reasons why two reputable practitioners considered it advisable to terminate. You were not alone in your judgement, Mr Parry.'

Up to this point Duncan had merely absorbed the fact that Ellen was dead, and that he, whom she had trusted, had failed her. Now, with Matron's last words, dawned the cold realization of the train of events that her death would inevitably set in motion, starting with the fact that, contrary to the requirements of the Abortion Act 1967, the operation had been undertaken with the sanction of only one doctor — the patient's lover, to boot! For the purposes of the official documentation, Duncan had used the name of a psychiatrist to whom he had referred one of his patients in the past, knowing there would be scant likelihood of his ever being asked to corroborate his mythical assessment of Ellen's mental condition. With her death 'scant likelihood' became 'certainty' and Duncan knew he was lost.

'There'll be an inquest.' He spoke his thought aloud.

Matron became businesslike. 'Yes. It'll have to be reported. I'd better instigate the procedure.' One hand hovered towards the telephone, the other drew a piece of paper which Duncan recognized as Ellen's consent form towards her. 'Next of kin,' she murmured, running a finger down the items.

'Her parents. I'll deal with them. I'd rather.' It was the least he could do for Ellen now. 'They're not at home. What address did she give?' Duncan stretched across the desk and looked at the space where Ellen had written her father's name and the Palmers Green address only yesterday. He didn't remember the name of the home to which they'd been sent. He didn't think Ellen had mentioned it. He thought for a moment. Her GP would most likely know. Dr Inglis had put her on to the Welfare people.

Duncan was wary in what he told the doctor when he got through, merely that there had been an accident and that he needed to know the whereabouts of the elderly Birches, and as he took down the name of the house and the street he wondered what would become of the old people now without Ellen's support. They should have been the ones to go — not she. There was nothing left for them but to become an inevitable burden upon the State, while she should have had everything to live for, untrammelled by them. God was untidy.

★ ★ ★

He took her things, which had been collected for him by a nurse, and put the shabby cardboard suitcase into his car. Out of a morbid sense of curiosity he'd opened the case when he was alone in Matron's office, and had turned back the few items it contained with his hand. There was a smock and a skirt, some plain underwear, shoes, tights, toilet items, a lipstick and a jar of cleanser and the nightgown Ellen had been wearing when he had examined her. They all smelled of her, a fresh smell of flower-scented soap which was more poignant than the articles themselves. She had never worn perfume like Frances, and he had not bought her any. He had given her few presents. Letters and gifts could be used against one if an affair became sour. Part of him was ashamed of his material and spiritual lack of generosity.

The familiar smell of a geriatric day room assailed Duncan on entering the lounge at The Hermitage. An amalgam of dried washing, incontinence and the halitosis of senility, served as a timely reminder that but for the grace of God this could be his own eventual destiny, prohibited an instinctive shudder. There were worse things than dying

64

young. The years would not condemn Ellen. There were three large circular tables in the room at which were seated a collection of men and women possessing varying degrees of animation. Some were playing board games, one assembled a jigsaw, some read or talked, while others just sat with their heads lolling between hunched shoulders, staring into space. Arranged around the walls the occupants of wheelchairs sat, taking in their surroundings or sleeping.

Duncan located Mr Birch sitting apart, reading his paper. He was thin and spruce with a tidily clipped moustache and the same short back and sides haircut he had affected in the Army sixty-five years before. His back was bent and the swollen deformities that held his *Telegraph* were the hands of the chronic arthritic, but his eyes were bright with intelligence and his deliberate isolation from the rest of the room indicated more powerfully than words his independence of it. Duncan introduced himself and sat down. For want of a better opening, he started, 'I'm a doctor,' but got no further before the old man interrupted him heatedly.

'I don't need another doctor. I've seen enough of them. Dr Inglis put me here in the first place. A home from home, he called it. Just the place for you while your

65

girl's away.' He snorted indignantly. 'Just the place for me! A loony-bin, that's what it is, and I may be old but I'm not ready for that yet. She may be — ' he jerked his head at a white-haired woman asleep with the other wallflowers and whom Duncan took to be his wife — 'but I'm not, and I'm getting out. Ellen should have known better.' He struggled to get up, but Duncan restrained him.

'It's about Ellen I've come. Please sit down. I'm afraid I've got some bad news for you.'

'About Ellen?' Mr Birch, arrested in rising, looked sharply at Duncan, then sank back into his chair. 'What is it?'

'I'm afraid she was taken ill, very ill. Nothing could be done. She's dead. She died today.' He repeated it in case the old man hadn't fully understood.

He looked bewildered. 'How can that be? She was all right yesterday. Bright as a button. An accident?'

'No, Mr Birch. Your daughter died in hospital today. She was admitted yesterday for an operation.' Duncan could see he didn't believe him.

'She was going away on business. That's why she put us in here. She shouldn't have. Mother perhaps, but I could have managed

66

at home. She went on business.'

'No,' Duncan insisted gently but firmly. 'She told you that but in fact she was going into hospital. She didn't want you to be worried. She was operated on today. There were complications. I'm afraid she died.'

The old man's eyes widened and darkened. Comprehension was there and the dawn of acceptance. His voice broke as he said, 'Ellen?' as if to make quite sure, and Duncan nodded and said again, 'I'm afraid so.' The twisted hands groped for a handkerchief in his cardigan sleeve. They were shaking, so Duncan proffered his own and waited while Mr Birch wiped the moisture from the corner of his eyes and nose. They sat in silence until he suddenly looked at Duncan and said, 'What operation?'

Having come thus far there was little point in sparing him. He had a right to know and anyway the report of the inquest would be in the press.

'I'm sorry to have to tell you this, but Ellen was pregnant. She was having an abortion.' There wasn't any way of wrapping it up prettily.

'Pregnant! Ellen?' Duncan could see he was finding momentary relief from grief in anger. 'She would never — not Ellen. She didn't know any men — only those at the office and they're all old. She was always making jokes about them. Making us laugh with her stories.' Memory returned and he broke off to blow his nose. He shook his head in incredulity. 'She couldn't have been pregnant, she couldn't. Unless — ' His eyes swivelled craftily to Duncan's face, then down. 'Who was the man? Do you know?'

'She didn't say.' For no good reason, Duncan felt apprehensive. He compelled himself to ask, 'Did she ever mention a name — anyone whom it might have been?'

'No. But there was a name once in her diary. She kept one, you know.' He eyed Duncan, defying his reproach for having read it. 'She left it lying about. I wouldn't have been human — ' He exonerated himself. 'A Scottish name. Andrew. Dougal. Something like that.' He creased his brows in an effort to remember.

'Probably nothing relevant.' Duncan tried to sound nonchalant. 'If she mentioned him only once. What did she say?' He had to know.

'I can't remember the exact words but something like — 'I spoke to — whatever his name was. I could see he was afraid for his career.' Words to that effect.' He thought a bit. 'Yes. Yes, you see what it could mean.'

He was sharp enough. Duncan's hopes hit rock bottom. 'I've got to get out of here. Must get home. I'll have his guts if it's the last thing I do. Ellen.' He fell to pondering on her name and now the tears coursed swiftly down his cheeks. Duncan called a nurse to his aid and escaped.

It had been foolish to imagine there might have been a loophole. Events were closing in upon him. With luck he had until the inquest, but between now and then there was no choice but to prepare Frances for what might lie ahead. He couldn't allow her to go into the court-room and learn about Ellen there, and nothing would keep her away from it once she knew he was in trouble. He drove home with a deep dread of inevitably impending doom.

★ ★ ★

After a couple of abortive attempts at conversation, Frances sat through the rest of supper in silence. She had been prepared in advance by Matron's phone call for Duncan to be strained and withdrawn. He had lost patients before, mercifully few, but when it happened there was always the same sense of impotence and fury of frustration to be exorcised, for which purpose he retired into his own private hell. If she were patient he would eventually talk it out of his system, so she waited, removing their plates between courses, forbearing to comment on his meagre appetite and abandoning the untouched pudding in favour of coffee which he drank down greedily before lighting his cigarette. The flint in his lighter failed to respond and he clicked it impatiently three or four times before it ignited. Frances noticed his hand was trembling and his face bent over the flame was pale and gaunt.

'Do you want — ?'

'Frances, I must — '

They both started speaking at the same instant, then stopped.

She said, 'Go on.'

'No. You.'

'I was going to ask if you wanted to talk about it?' She waited while he fiddled with his spoon in his saucer. He finally looked at her.

'Yes, we must.'

'Only if you want to.'

'I don't want to. I wasn't going to. But now I must.' He turned his fist into the palm of his hand and cracked the knuckles. 'Frances, do you love me?'

A preliminary shaft of unease assailed her. 'You know I do.'

'And I love you. I want you to remember that. What I'm going to tell you doesn't change that.'

Unease turned to positive fear. It was the sort of thing people said when they were going to hurt you badly. Frances sat expectantly still, not allowing herself to imagine what form the confession would take. Instinct told her that this was what had been hanging over her head since the night of the dinner-party. When it came, haltingly at first, baldly describing his meetings with Ellen, the fact that they were lovers, the break-up of the relationship and the subsequent news of the pregnancy, she remained stunned and silent, anticipating the worst that was yet to come. He told her plainly without embellishment or excuse, his voice gathering momentum and strength as he continued, as by consigning his burden to her, he lifted the isolation of his hitherto solitary confinement. When he stopped speaking Frances felt numb, sick and lost. The silence between them lengthened as he waited for her bitter censure, recriminations, her reaffirmation of her love for him, her understanding — her reaction whatever it might be, but there were too many shock aspects in his revelation for her to be able to analyse instantly her feelings. Her first question was a practical one.

'Can they send you to prison for what you've done?'

'Can, and will. I have procured an illegal abortion.'

'So there'll be a trial?' Frances saw his look of shame and self-abnegation. 'I'm not trying to tread you into the ground. I want the very worst that can happen to be spelled out. I want to know what we're up against. Don't pull any punches.'

He recalled Ellen's 'Thanks for saying 'we'.' A small corner of his miserable heart warmed. 'There'll be legal proceedings, a trial, imprisonment. Three years is the normal stint. There'll also be a hearing of the GMC. I shall be struck off. There won't be any money coming in. How's that for starters?' Her courage made him brutal. 'Oh, it doesn't seem fair. People get away with suspended sentences on murder charges, bank robberies. Why, just because I'm a doctor — ' Duncan spread his arms in a hopeless gesture of self-pity. He went on more quietly. 'The suggestion may be made that I was deliberately negligent. That she was too much of an embarrassment.'

'And was she?'

'God no! You should know me better than that.'

'I thought I did.'

72

'Besides — she's far worse trouble to me dead in these circumstances. What am I going to do, Fran?' The long nightmare of the day culminating in the present exchange with Frances undid him. He dropped his head into his hands, breaking down completely. She let him sob. Her own eyes felt dry and gritty, her mouth arid, her knees decidedly wobbly as she went away to refill the coffee-pot because it was something to do. When he had blown his noise and got himself under control she said:

'You must have loved her very much to have taken such risks — putting your career and us in the balance.'

Duncan shook his head. 'No. No I didn't.' How could he possibly make her understand? 'It wasn't love. Not our sort of love — on either side.'

'What was it, then? I don't think I can bear it if you say it was 'just one of those things'. You're not like that.' Had he been, he would have been a more imaginative lover. She stifled the disloyalty and was thankful that in shocked acrimony she had not given it tongue.

'It's crazy, but that's just what it was. It was only a few times. It had been over months ago. She was lonely, rather pathetic, expected nothing much from life, needed comfort. She made me feel protective — strong.'

Frances swallowed hard. 'Was that so necessary?'

He smiled at her wistfully. 'You're a strong person, Fran. You don't need my protection. The boot is on the other foot with us.'

'That seemed to be the way you wanted it. You're saying that I emasculate you?'

'I didn't mean to hurt anybody.' The age-old cry. She wanted to hit him.

'How could you be such a bloody fool? For someone who doesn't want to hurt people you've got an impeccable track record. David. Ellen. Your child. Me.' The words were dragged out of her bitterness, a sense of personal failure and deep injustice. 'I wish you'd told me earlier.'

'About Ellen? It wouldn't have been necessary. I told you, Fran, it meant nothing.'

'About the baby.'

'What good would it have done?'

'We might have kept it. It would have been better than — ' She couldn't continue for the rush of tears in her throat and behind her eyes. The hideous criminal unfairness of life momentarily defeated her. He reached out to touch her but she ignored the gesture.

He said, 'I'm truly sorry that part of it is so painful, Fran.'

'Yes — well.' She blew her nose and squared her shoulders. Her salvation lay in thinking positively. 'It's no good looking back. The immediate thing is, are you quite certain things are as bad as they seem? There may not be a prosecution. Can't you cover up?'

He shook his head. 'No chance. Ellen's diary will prove I was her lover. The certificate I signed naming the psychiatrist is a forgery.'

She stared at him, unbelieving. 'God, what a mess!'

'I know I deserve anything you may say. I don't deserve your help.'

'I can't help you this time, Duncan.' She could see his surprise and fear and knew he had misunderstood her. 'Oh, I'm not leaving you or anything dramatic like that. But you need qualified expert advice.' She had to admit it. 'You need Bernard. You'd better get on to him, but before he comes, is there anything else — anything worse — that I should know?'

He smiled grimly. 'What could be worse?'

She couldn't imagine, but no doubt in the days ahead, she would find out.

# 6

She did, and Frances also discovered that being prepared for it in no way made it less distasteful when it actually happened. In her heart she had cherished the hope that Duncan had exaggerated the gravity of his position, and as the days leading up to the inquest passed uneventfully, with him carrying out his normal routine and life proceeding on the surface as usual, she began to believe that the consequences he had feared had been greatly magnified by his guilty imagination.

Bernard had taken the legal angle into his capable hands. Leading Duncan once again through his story in front of Frances, and then alone, his attitude had been totally professional and objective, evincing neither shocked horror, disbelief nor embarrassment, and by his businesslike approach, steadying Duncan by defusing the situation emotionally. Listening to him at work, Frances began to understand the ingredients of his success. She had managed to engineer a moment alone with him as he had stepped into his car, when he had given it to her straight. 'It's going to take more than you or I can do to bail him out of this one, Fran.'

★ ★ ★

The day before the inquest Dr Inglis rang Duncan with the unpleasant news that Mr Birch had given him a letter to be delivered to the Coroner.

'The old boy can't attend himself, but he's told me the gist, and I think I ought to warn you he's making some pretty outrageous allegations against yourself. Although you didn't do me the courtesy of informing me of my patient's condition, Parry, I feel we professional men owe each other a degree of *esprit de corps*.' His cold disapproval communicated itself across the wire.

'It's all I can expect,' said Duncan when he repeated the conversation to Frances. 'Bernard has told me how it will be. He hasn't pulled any punches.'

She was suddenly frightened for the first time. The reality of the future was advancing too quickly. She had a sense of time running out for them too rapidly and she wanted to hold him. He had made no physical overtures to her since the night of his confession, and though they had lain side by side in the double bed, both had withdrawn into their own mental fastness. Now all she wanted was to assure, to be reassured before it was too late. That night she put her hand across and touched him. He stiffened and she thought he would repulse her, but then he turned towards her and came into her arms. They didn't speak, but held each other in the tenderness of consolation, his face between her breasts, her hand caressing the back of his head and gently pressing him to her. Presently she felt him harden and she opened herself to him to give him the comfort of her body.

★ ★ ★

After that followed a period of unadulterated hell. The train of events set in motion by Mr Birch's discovery that the Christian name of his daughter's lover happened to be the same as that of the doctor who had visited him on the day of her death, the one who had performed the actual operation, chugged its inevitable way through his complaint to the Coroner and the General Medical Council, an adjourned inquest and police investigations. Duncan answered all their questions politely and without prevarication and on the hideous day that he was arrested and charged with manslaughter he allowed

78

himself to be led away with dignity and a calm acceptance. He had not wanted Frances to go with him to the police station.

'Don't worry,' he repeated fruitlessly and inanely. 'They won't keep me in at this juncture.' He looked towards the detective-inspector who was waiting tactfully while they made their parting. The latter cleared his throat.

'Probably not longer than one night, sir. You'll have to appear before the Magistrates tomorrow morning, then I dare say you'll be released on bail pending trial.'

'Bail? You'll need sureties. Me, of course. Who else? Your parents?'

Duncan winced. He had put off telling his parents and now the news would perforce come from Frances. It was too late for him to hope this would not be construed by them as cowardice on his part. He swallowed hard.

'Will you get in touch with them?'

Frances nodded her head which felt as if it were stuffed with cotton-wool. Nothing was quite real. 'Leave everything to me. I'd better pack a bag for you.' She ran upstairs and got a grip, making an effort to concentrate upon what had to go into it. Standing helplessly in the bathroom, surveying a shelf of toilet requisites, her shocked state of mind rendered her incapable of selection. Pulling herself together, she put in what Duncan would need for one night and took the bag downstairs. 'What time tomorrow morning?' she asked the inspector.

'Ten o'clock, madam.'

She turned to Duncan. 'I'll be there, darling. I'll be there with Bernard.'

★ ★ ★

He had been released on bail of £5000 the next day. 'And two sureties of the same figure,' the magistrate intoned, making a note on his papers. Duncan looked as if he had been awake all night when he and Bernard joined Frances and his father outside the court-room. Alistair Parry had made the journey from Sussex that morning and had spoken only briefly to Frances before the hearing. She had relayed the bare bones of Duncan's circumstances to him over the phone the previous night and had been thankful for his calm acceptance of the facts and the communication of his support for them both in spite of his shocked condition. He looked thin and strained but perfectly in command of himself as he shook hands with his son, who said quickly, 'Thanks for coming, Dad.'

Alistair turned to Bernard. In the split

second before the two men nodded their acknowledgement of one another, Frances imagined she momentarily detected a frostiness in the atmosphere, which seconds later she dismissed as due to her perceptions being over-heightened by anxiety.

'Sir Alistair.' Bernard inclined his head. 'I haven't had an opportunity to congratulate you on the title. How are you? And Lady Parry?'

'Quite well, thank you, Bernard.'

There was a small silence, filled in by Duncan asking Bernard, 'What happens next?'

'You'll be committed for trial, probably in about six weeks' time. It could be longer, but as you're pleading guilty things will be able to be expedited more quickly. You'll have to appear for committal proceedings on a date to be named, when you'll be committed to the Central Criminal Court of the Old Bailey for trial.' In spite of trying to make it sound like the outline for a perfectly normal course of events, his words sounded to Frances terrifyingly official.

'How long will I get?'

'It hasn't got that far,' Alistair Parry interposed.

'How long?' Duncan persisted. 'Three years?'

Bernard glanced quickly at Frances. 'It could be — but you won't serve that. You'd get a third off for good behaviour automatically. More likely you'd be released on licence after eighteen months.'

'A year and a half.' It sounded even longer when calculated that way, Frances thought.

★ ★ ★

Duncan had never known six weeks to hang fire so dismally. If six weeks in the comfort of his own home could feel like six months, how was he to bear a year and a half in prison?

'You won't be behind bars,' Bernard had assured him. 'It'll be an open prison.'

It was some relief to know that. 'So long as they give me plenty to do,' was his perpetual prayer. At present, at home, suspended from his work by the General medical Council who awaited the findings of the trial before instituting their own enquiry, time hung heavily. There were business matters to be arranged to enable Frances to carry on alone throughout his absence, the details of which they discussed, prominent among which figured the sale of the house. Duncan had registered a token resistance to the calm acceptance by Frances that it must go, but they both knew that it was inevitable. Apart from being too large and expensive to run for Frances on her own, there was the future to be considered and they had to look forward to the time when Duncan, on release, would be looking for a job. The remote chance that he might not be sentenced to prison did not detract from the inevitability of his being struck off. Whatever happened, his income at best would be greatly reduced, at worst non-existent, and the money from Hill House and any interest accrued would be necessary to finance whatever new start his rehabilitation occasioned.

Frances had decided her best plan would be to try to find herself a flat or small house to rent, if such a thing were possible. That way, the realized capital on the house would remain untouched and she could pay her way on what she made out of the business.

'My needs won't be extravagant and if I bought a property it might not fill our requirements later. I can always bunk up with Liz over the shop if I can't find something immediately. She's offered. So has Dolly, but I'm not going to be caught that way.'

'You're so well organized it'll be funny if I don't get sent down.'

She determinedly ignored his sarcasm. 'Then we shall be able to buy something that suits us both, shan't we?'

Grudgingly he admired her forward thinking, yet illogically he resented the way in which she assumed the initiative, as if he were already safely out of the way, he told himself. These sentiments goaded him into making a private arrangement with Bernard over the organization of the money when realized, which he divulged to Frances as a virtual *fait accompli* when it was all but sewn up.

She returned from the shop the evening before the trial to find Bernard with Duncan in the study, some papers spread before them on the desk, poring over a sheet of pencilled figures. Duncan looked up at her entry.

'Come here, Fran. This will need your signature if things go as we expect tomorrow. I've signed my bit.'

'What is it?' She came across and looked at the paper, trying to make some sense of the calculations. 'It looks Greek to me — but then I'm not the world's greatest mathematician.'

'That's what I told Bernard and that's why we think it would be best if he took all this off your hands. You're going to have plenty on your plate with the shop and finding a place to live and being responsible for everything I'll have dumped on you.'

'All what?'

Bernard came to stand by her side. 'It's a plan for making your capital work for you in the best possible way. Look, here's the figure you've accepted for the house — £150,000. That cheque should be through in a few days. After mortgage repayment here,' he drew his index finger across the sheet, 'and fees on sale, here, let's say you should have £122,500 roughly to play around with. You'll want to invest in maximum of non-taxable funds — Savings Certificates, say £1000 each, National Savings Bank, say £1400 each, Premium Bonds, £2000 each, Save As You Earn at £40 per month each. If you did that to start with, you'd be left with this figure.' His elbow came down to his side as he lowered the pointing finger and their shoulders and arms touched. Her head bent, Frances's concentration veered from the numbers to an acute consciousness of his physical presence. His arm, through the worsted of his sleeve, felt steel hard, the elbow sharp, and was it her imagination or did he lean into her ever so slightly to emphasize the contact? The hairs on the nape of her neck tingled and alarmingly her nipples tautened. She took a step away from him. 'Now this, I advise you to spread between Gilts,' he was saying, 'free of Capital

Gains Tax, and Equities. I could advise you on these.'

'Someone would have to,' Frances joked.

'Exactly.' Duncan was ready to make his point. 'It isn't an area with which you're totally familiar, Fran, to say the least. Bernard has very kindly offered to administer a Trust fund for us if we are agreeable. It would mean you wouldn't have to worry and with his knowledge of the market he'd know what shares to choose, etcetera. I'd be a lot happier.'

Frances said slowly, 'It would seem like a good idea.' She needed time to grasp it and was faintly annoyed that Duncan hadn't seen fit to discuss it with her by herself. Here, in Bernard's presence, it would appear churlish to raise any objection, not that she could find a valid one, just an unreasonable reluctance to consign any part of her destiny to him. It was not as if he were not absolutely trustworthy. Uncannily, as though reading her thoughts, Bernard said:

'Naturally I shouldn't be the sole administrator. You remember George Bruton — my partner. You met him once, I believe. He'd be co-trustee so there'd be no scope for any skulduggery.' He smiled straight into her eyes and she hoped her discomfiture was not obvious. Frances cast her mind back to the occasion on which she had encountered Bernard's partner. She had previously heard much of him as a butt of Bernard's jokes against the rigid establishment of the Law. George was the epitome of the senior partner nearing retirement, a pillar of his local church, prominent on the local council, wrapped up in numerous good works and as morally incorruptible as the figure of Justice herself.

'I'd only exact a nominal fee — dinner now and again — nothing too extravagant.' His eyes mocked her, and now she knew he had deliberately touched her earlier as they lingered on her mouth like a melodramatic warning that he'd like to exact payment of a more disturbing kind.

'That's enormously kind of you, Bernard. Isn't it, Fran?' Duncan seemed unconscious of her hesitancy. 'You've taken a weight off my mind.'

'Glad to. Perhaps if you'll sign here, Fran.'

Unable to find a reason not to do so, Frances signed her name.

'That's it,' said Bernard, pocketing the document. 'Of course if it's good news tomorrow — we tear this up. That goes without saying. Let's hope we can.'

★ ★ ★

It was a relief when the next day dawned. The
past weeks had been a strain with, apart from
business, no subjects of normal conversation
left to pursue. Without Duncan's work to
talk about or any definite future to plan
for, Frances's main topic had been the
shop and its expansion of business, but
she soon realized that hers and Liz's success
made him feel the more inadequate, so this
theme too died. The stress on them both
of weighing and considering what could be
spoken without in some way hurting the
other became intolerably wearisome and
they lapsed into uncommunicative silence.
Only at night, holding each other for
solace between the sheets, did they unite
of necessity, but even their love-making
was conducted without words, and that
eventually failed them as well as, with
tension mounting, Duncan found to his
disgust his capabilities dwindling. Now his
humiliation was complete.

Frances sat in the court with her in-laws
and Liz and listened to the verdict as forecast
by Bernard. She was allowed to see Duncan
in the cells below the dock for a brief
moment before he was taken away. She was
so determined not to cry that speech was an

impossibility, so she held him in her arms and kissed him goodbye with an intensity that, instead of comforting him, embarrassed him under the eye of the watchful warder. There were reporters on the pavement when they came out and photographers who ran with them to the car and kept on flashing their bulbs until Alistair drove off.

'Disgusting. Like vultures.' Amelia, thin-lipped, brushed specks impatiently from her coat as if she could at the same time rid herself of the unwelcome publicity the members of the press represented. With the iron self-discipline of a lifetime, she had paid as much attention to her dress and make-up today as always, yet under the rouge her cheeks had hollowed and there was a puffiness beneath the carefully mascaraed eyes. Her rigidity repelled any gesture of comfort. Frances was very grateful at that moment for Liz's hand which crept silently down to grasp her own where it lay between them on the back seat of the car.

★ ★ ★

She had laid on lunch for the four of them back at Hill House, Bernard having remained with his client to tie up some details, then being required back at his office to deal with matters he had interrupted in order to be in court.

'I'll be round this evening,' he had promised Frances at the conclusion of the nightmare, and she had tried to thank him but there had been no available words.

It was a difficult meal, partaken of by Amelia in silence and by the rest of them in an impossible attempt to render the situation normal by superficial conversation. Towards the end of it Alistair enquired gently when Frances was moving.

'I've got a fortnight's leeway before I have to get out. I'm moving in with Liz for a week or two. I'll store the furniture. Hopefully it won't be for too long. I don't want to fritter away the proceeds from the house on unnecessary storage charges.'

Alistair cleared his throat. 'I know you're very capable, Frances, and you'll take due consideration before making any investment. I should like to be of help if you feel consultation with me would be useful.'

Frances smiled at him gratefully. 'Thank you. Of course I shall come to you if I need to. Fortunately, Bernard is such a whizz kid and knows all about our affairs, being Duncan's solicitor, that I hope I shan't have to bother you too much.'

Alistair wiped his mouth carefully. 'Sometimes it is useful to have a second opinion. An older head. You want to be sure you know what you're doing, my dear.' The gaze he bent upon her was curiously significant, as though he were saying one thing and intending to convey an altogether different meaning — a warning? Frances was touched he should be so patently solicitous for her. She reached across the table and pressed his hand.

'I appreciate your offer, and your concern for me.'

The shrewd eyes under the grey brows blurred with moisture and her father-in-law suddenly looked very tired and old. This business had knocked hell out of him, she thought. Frances realized with a shock other signs of wear and tear about his appearance, thrown into sharp relief by the ageing droop of his shoulders and the lines of fatigue the day had etched upon the once proud features. The cuffs of his shirt jacket were a little frayed, the material worn shiny round the buttonholes. His tie was held in place by an ill-concealed safety-pin instead of the customary gold bar, and the arm of his spectacles was temporarily mended with a piece of sticking plaster. 'Shabby genteel' was a phrase no one would hitherto have dreamed of applying to Alistair Parry. Such evidences of decay touched Frances strangely and frighteningly. Subconsciously she relied upon Alistair as a personal champion and friend. Looking at him now, she realized that the time was approaching when he would need to be saved from stress rather than have her troubles foisted upon him.

★ ★ ★

She said as much to Bernard when he arrived later in the evening. Until his coming the house had seemed very empty and quiet as Frances had moved from room to room, mentally stripping each one of furniture and memories. A great deal of the former and most of the latter would have to go. She set her mind against remembering the happiness she had known here, since so much of it had proved apparently to be in her own imagination. By his own admission, Duncan had not been content with the status quo of their marriage. Had he been, would he have sought the comfort of Ellen? In spite of all his denials Frances had failed him. The doorbell interrupted her reverie and she ran downstairs to admit Bernard.

He stepped over the threshold armed with his briefcase and a bottle of champagne.

'A little pick-me-up, Fran. I thought you might need one.' He surveyed her. 'I can see you do.'

'Thank you. I felt ghastly before, now I know I look worse.'

'Never ghastly. Just very tired.' Disposing of his case, he kissed her forehead chastely.

Frances laughed. 'Always honest.'

'Nearly always.' He enjoyed the way her face broke up as she smiled. 'That's better. Where are the glasses? Let's drink to the ending of this perfectly bloody day.'

After the second glass she felt better. They were sitting in Duncan's study in front of a glowing fire and Frances felt herself relaxing for the first time for what seemed like weeks, letting the warmth of the drink and the coals seep into her cramped muscles. 'You're sure he was all right?' she asked him for the third time.

'He was in good heart, Fran. More anxious about you than about himself. He sent you all his love and said he knew he didn't have to tell you to be brave.'

She said nothing. No. Duncan would expect nothing less of her.

'Are you going to be all right here tonight?'

'I'm not in the mood to cut my throat, if that's what you mean.'

'A pity. I was hoping to have the excuse to

stay with you, although on second thoughts, to seduce you immediately would show a certain lack of delicacy.'

She laughed again. 'It was kind of you to think of it, all the same.'

He raised his eyebrows. 'Seduction?'

'No. Me being here alone. To tell you the truth, it's a relief after what's been going on. His going — it'll give us time. Neither of us could be normal with each other. Too much had happened. Ellen — and the baby.' A shadow crossed her face. 'Everything that's happened has shown up our marriage in a different light. I need time to get acclimatized.'

'Then what?'

'I don't know. Obviously we can't go on the same. That wasn't apparently satisfactory for him, yet how can I change? People don't, do they?'

'I hope not.' The banter had gone out of his voice and he was looking at her in a way that made her feel undressed.

She turned the conversation. 'I don't know how to thank you for all you've done, Bernard. We're very fortunate in our friends. You and Liz — and Alistair — have helped so much. I hope it'll make Duncan see his father in a different light. He's got such a chip about them — understandable in

94

Amelia's case, but all this has hit Alistair really badly. He was so sweet to me today. To tell you the truth, I'm quite a bit worried about him. He looked so aged and somehow down-at-heel — almost letting himself go to seed. Amelia doesn't notice anyone but herself and he runs in circles round her and there's no one to worry about him. It was rather pathetic. Had you noticed?'

'Can't say that I had.' Bernard swung one leg over the other and lifted the champagne bottle off the table between them. 'Have some more.' He filled her glass.

'Don't you ever go down to Falconers now?'

'Not a lot. We're in touch from time to time.'

'Did you notice how run-down the place is getting? Do you suppose there could be a shortage of cash?'

'If there is, that's his problem, Fran. You've got enough of your own.'

She was surprised by his seeming callousness. 'You're very detached. I thought they meant a lot to you.'

'They've certainly done so in the past. They've meant more to me than anyone will ever know.' He looked down into his glass and swirled the bubbles with his finger. There was a far-away expression on his face.

She pressed her point. 'I think Alistair would like it if you found time to go and see them more often.'

He lifted his eyes and regarded her thoughtfully. 'Do you, Frances? Well then, I probably shall.'

His promise partially relieved her, but in the days that followed anxiety for Duncan's father faded in the fullness of her own life.

# 7

There was little to distinguish No. 6 Ullswater Road from its grey, stuccoed two-up, two-down neighbours, with their front-room bay windows, single-gabled roofs and stained glass insets on either side of the porch. Detached, with a minuscule front garden and a long, narrow, fenced plot at the back, its anonymous uniformity suited Frances after the public singularity of her position of late. No. 6 was a haven to which she could retire to lick her wounds, where her neighbours knew nothing about her and, she hoped, would care less. The cul-de-sac finished where a piece of green waste land commenced. It was a handy open space used by children to ride their bicycles and by the inhabitants of Ullswater and the adjacent Windermere and Coniston Roads to exercise their dogs. It also provided a less claustrophobic atmosphere to a closely built-up area. Whoever had named the roads had either been unacquainted with the Lake District, or had done so out of a perverse sense of humour. They were unadopted and un-made-up and their pot-holes and craters presented a formidable obstacle to low-slung chassis, becoming muddied lagoons after a day of rain.

Frances had been fortunate in being able to rent the house unfurnished. Originally the owner, an engineer whose job had moved temporarily to the Persian Gulf, had been loath to lease it to her empty for fear of not being able to move her out again on his return. Bernard's eloquent explanation that the house was only required for the duration of Duncan's sentence (the length of which happily coincided with the owner's overseas assignment), together with some judicious withers-wringing concerning his client's pitiful situation, finally persuaded the engineer in Frances's favour. He, in turn, screwed his storage costs out of the Arabs and a conclusion was reached satisfactory to everyone.

The remainder of Hill House's effects that couldn't be accommodated by the sitting-room at the back or the three upstairs bedrooms, Frances had stacked into the bow-windowed front room overlooking the street. In the end she had disposed of very little. Some fitted carpets and curtains had been cut down to fit No. 6, the rest had been sold with the house. A private buyer had taken Duncan's Bentley. Seeing it in the garage had upset Frances almost more than anything else. She had never driven it. It was so much a part of him and daily she expected to see him getting out of it after his rounds, or to hear its engine starting up in the morning. She smiled ruefully, imagining the minor sensation behind net curtains the Bentley would create negotiating the assault course of Ullswater Road.

Liz and she had made fun of moving-day, but Dolly's sensibilities had been offended by Frances's choice. 'You can't mean to live here, Fran. I mean — the district!' She scanned the other houses with contempt and sighed. 'You're so pigheaded. We could have had a much more suitable place together. Even my flat is better than this.'

'You can always visit me under cover of dark,' said Frances with amused sarcasm.

'Whatever would Duncan say?' said Dolly, temporarily forgetting Duncan's own inauspicious housing arrangements. 'Still — ' dubiously — 'I suppose you have to do what you think is right.' Her tone implied that one learned from one's mistakes.

'You won't know it when it's finished and I've got the garden under way. I shall divide it with a path, have a rock-garden at the end, vegetables here and roses, then clematis and climbers to cover the fence.'

'It'll be hard going. I shouldn't think this soil has got much life in it.' Dolly inspected the plot, thick with couch grass and flattened, trampled weeds. 'I hope you're not going to cut yourself off from all your friends.'

'Any that want to can find me here. The others won't matter. Bernard thinks I've done the right thing.'

'Does he?' Dolly gave her an old-fashioned look. 'I suppose Bernard might.'

Frances looked at her sharply. 'And what does that mean?'

'Nothing. Except I can see it might suit Bernard to have you tucked away down here on your own, whereas living with me you would be chaperoned. It hasn't escaped me he's been pretty much in evidence.'

Frances whitened with anger. 'Bernard has been a marvellous friend to both of us and Duncan encourages me to ask for his help.'

It was true. Since going to prison Duncan had delegated all his responsibilities to Bernard. As if acclimatizing himself to his changed situation in life was all that he could presently cope with, it was as though he could hardly be bothered with the alien business matters of that other world of which he was no longer a part. Bernard had duly invested the proceeds from the sale of Hill House as directed, furnishing Frances with a list of securities and amounts involved and been instrumental in finding No. 6.

The decorations in the house were inoffensive and in good enough repair for Frances to live with, and although No. 6 was small and situated in a down-grade district, it was far from squalid as Dolly had implied. In fact it had an atmosphere of cosy, well-built solidity to which Frances attached more importance than to its unfavourable exterior. The sitting-room had taken the smaller of her sofas and two armchairs, a china cabinet and a couple of occasional tables as well as a folding D-end wall table that could be opened out and used for dining purposes. Frances had kept out only a few favourite ornaments and a pair of shortened brocade curtains from Hill House hung at the french window. Like the back downstairs room that she had decided to use as her living-room, the kitchen looked over the garden and its yellow and white paint had come up clean and bright after she had washed its walls and ceiling. Upstairs there was a double bedroom, a minute single one and a bathroom just large enough to turn round in while drying. The largest room was north facing on to the road. Frances's pink chintz curtains and bedspread diffused its harsher light and the deep rose carpet lent it a necessary warmth.

It came as a surprise to find how little time she had to feel lonely. She missed Duncan horribly but not nearly so much as she had when surrounded by constant reminders of his absence. At No. 6 all his clothes and impedimenta were packed in the front room and, apart from his photograph beside her bed and another of their wedding downstairs, the house exuded solely her personality. Besides, there was so much to do that there was little time for reflecting soulfully on the past, and by the end of each day she was tired enough to drop into bed and sink straight into sleep. There were occasions when the small hours found her wakeful and a prey to doubts and imaginings, wondering if Duncan too were lying awake with sadness and longing, conscious of the cold void in the bed beside her, but these times in the pit became rarer and when they occurred she would get up and make herself a hot drink, concentrating upon the business of the day ahead until the warmth of the toddy soothed her.

Time was punctuated by her fortnightly visits to Duncan. Every other Sunday she would drive down to Sussex to the open prison where he had been sent, and they spent the afternoon together. The visits were a strain on them both, during which they lapsed into the stilted conversation of strangers unacquainted with each other's world, struggling to find a point of contact. The first time it had been a shock that she had been unable to distinguish him at once from his companions as they came into the recreation room set with tables like a cafeteria, round which knots of families and friends awaited them. In his regulation prison dress of grey trousers, blue and white striped shirt, jacket and tie he looked almost nondescript, though she had never thought of him as ordinary before. All the same, the cut and fit and general impression of the uniform were better than she had anticipated. She said as much.

'What did you expect? Broad arrows?'

'I didn't know what to expect.'

'How could you?' He was quiet for a moment.

She said lightly, 'Well, it's hardly Savile Row but it's better than I feared.'

He fingered his tie. 'These are doled out to make us look respectable for visitors. I hand it back when you go. On the same principle we aren't allowed laces.' He thrust out his feet towards her to show her a pair of black slip-on shoes.

'Are you going to be warm enough?'

'I want for nothing. You're fully equipped when you come in here. Vests, pants, socks, pyjamas, a pullover. There's nothing I need.' His mouth twisted bitterly. 'Are you all right? Not that I'm any use to you if you're not.'

'I'm fine.' She had smiled, brightly reassuring. Sitting with him, alone amid a room of strangers, she felt constrained and distant. It was a lot easier in letters. She tried to draw him out to talk about the work he had been allocated in the library and the prison conservatory, books she had brought for him to read, television programmes — anything to keep the dialogue between them going, but his replies to her questions were brief, if not monosyllabic, and she couldn't decide whether he was being deliberately difficult or if his attitude was symptomatic of a deeper depression. She spoke about this to the prison doctor who told her that there was nothing to worry about and that Duncan would adjust, but she remained unhappy and drained after their times together. She learned not to swamp him with her own doings, the minutiae of which afforded him more cause for resentment than entertainment, and as she felt their points of contact diminishing, simultaneously she became more apprehensive.

★ ★ ★

There had been one grisly day in London when Duncan had been hauled up under escort to face his hearing at the General Medical Council. Although the result of the proceedings was a foregone conclusion, hearing it actually pronounced by his peers that he was to be struck off the register 'having committed a criminal offence and having had intercourse with a patient', signified to Duncan a more profound disgrace even than had his trial and the resulting sentence. He would be debarred from practising for at least five years. That meant that he could not hope to be reinstated until three years after he came out of prison. In blind panic he couldn't begin to think of what he might do. Medicine had been all his life.

'I shall be lucky to be flogging french letters. Isn't that what most of the unfrocked quacks do?'

He had been allowed to speak to Frances before the hearing and he prayed that there would be a few seconds afterwards that they could have together privately. It was therefore with some misgiving that on emerging from his ordeal he recognized his parents waiting outside on a seat in the hall.

'Glad to have this chance of seeing you, my boy. How are you?' Alistair patted his son awkwardly on the shoulder.

'I'm well, thank you,' Duncan said stiffly. 'Mother.' He turned to Amelia and kissed her cheek. Her eyes darted beyond his shoulder scouting for photographers, and, seeing none, she allowed herself to be embraced.

'We were in town and thought Frances might like company for lunch today,' Alistair said.

'That's good of you.' Duncan was grateful. He could sense his escort getting restive to be off. 'Thank you for all your letters.' He faced Frances. 'Goodbye, Fran.'

Unmindful of the prison officers, she held him in her arms.

'Goodbye, darling. I'll see you a week on Sunday.' She kissed him on the mouth, her lips quivering, and then they took him away.

'Well, that's that.' Amelia pulled on her gloves, smoothing the wrinkles down her fingers. 'A brilliant career down the drain. I'll never understand my son. He's had every advantage, every encouragement, a family with a high tradition of service and honour — all thrown away because of a tuppeny-ha'penny girl. You must have known about her, Frances. Couldn't you see what was happening?'

'I had no idea.'

'Then you should have, that's all I can say. A wife can always tell, if she's doing her own job properly. It was a mistake not having a family. A man needs security and responsibility, something to bind him.'

Frances said faintly, 'I won't stop for lunch if you don't mind. I have to get back to work.'

Alistair looked embarrassed. 'You'll let us know if you need anything?'

'Yes, of course,' Frances lied. She managed to get away and hurried towards the tube. Some people on the escalator saw her crying and looked away quickly.

★ ★ ★

Life was hectic at home and at the shop. Business had taken an unexpected lift, lurching into a boom, to keep pace with which both women had to work flat out. As a result of Frances's determined hawking them from store to store, a line of accessories designed by herself in materials printed by Liz had impressed a large London retailer who had placed orders for as many as they could make. In order to fulfil this and their other commitments, they took on two extra hands.

'Any minute now we shall have to do a

Laura Ashley,' said Liz gaily. 'Move out into the country and buy our own factory.'

'The lease of the premises next door would do for starters. I see it's up for sale and we could use the extra space. We're going to need more helpers and somewhere to house them, a bigger stock-room. If this continues we should be able to raise the cash, although it might be a flash in the pan. Don't bank on the private jet just yet!' All the same, as the figures crept up it was gratifying to be able to live on her share of the profits, knowing that the interest on the money from Hill House was accruing for the unpredictable future.

Within two more months they were both thankful they had taken the gamble in bidding for the vacant lease. The individuality of their range had immediately attracted interest once it had hit the wider market. The goods had been snapped up and re-orders from the original retailer, together with enquiries from others both in London and further afield, were coming in to the office in a steady stream. Late into the night they sat up drawing up specifications that Bernard, who knew somebody in the planning department, managed to get hustled through for the re-building to start at the earliest possible moment.

'Your Bernard's a handy person to know,'

commented Liz. 'Does the string exist that he can't pull?'

'He wouldn't admit it.' Frances laughed. 'He enjoys manipulating events.'

'And people, I shouldn't wonder.' Her tone was dry enough to make Frances look at her keenly.

'I thought you liked him.'

'I can't help myself doing that. I don't know that I completely trust him.'

'In business?' Frances experienced a prick of alarm.

'Mm — no.' Liz pursed her lips. 'Woman-wise — but that's probably because he's a man. I'm jaundiced.'

'You trusted Duncan.'

'Which proves my fallibility? You could be right.' She sounded unconvinced.

'Duncan and I used to think you two might make a good match.'

'Bernard and I? Whatever gave you that idea? Besides, he's a confirmed bachelor and I've learned enough not to put my head into that noose again.'

'Not ever?'

'Certainly not with Bernard,' Liz said definitely. 'Does that relieve you?' she asked slyly.

'Why should it?' Frances feigned nonchalant surprise.

'Come off it, Fran. I know you fancy him. He's fancied you for as long as I've known him. Probably long before that.'

'What makes you say that?'

'You know it.' Liz's amber eyes smiled lazily. Frances carefully shaded in a square on the plan before her.

'Don't be ridiculous.'

'Nobody could blame you if you did something about it. Least of all Duncan, but then he would never know. Eighteen months is a long time to do without it.'

Frances resumed her pencilling of the diagram. 'You seem to manage.'

Liz blew out the smoke from a recently lit cigarette. 'I've been inoculated. It's never meant that much to me. That's probably why that bastard left me, if I'm truthful. But you're different — too loving and warm. It'll be harder for you.'

Concentrating on the project on the graph paper, Frances said:

'We can have an extra square foot of shelving in either the work-room or the store. Come here and tell me which it is to be.'

# 8

The night before Duncan's next visiting day, Frances received a phone call from Bernard asking if he might accompany her to the prison.

'I don't want to butt in on any intimate tête-à-tête,' he was at pains to assure her, 'but I've got the answers to one or two legal queries he made and I'd only take ten minutes of his time at the most. I can sit in the car or take a walk until you're ready to come home.'

Frances, secretly relieved, accepted his suggestion readily. She had been down with Bernard on two former occasions and had found that his presence had a leavening effect upon the atmosphere of the visit, reducing its tension and making Duncan try harder to project some interest into the proceedings. It was pleasant, too, to have company on the journey there and back and Frances's spirits, normally apprehensive before visiting day, rose perceptibly.

'I'll treat you to lunch on the way. Pick you up at eleven-thirty,' he promised before ringing off.

* * *

He was as good as his word, but then
punctuality was all part of Bernard's reliability.
How many times had she hung around
for Duncan, dressed and ready for some
occasion at which they would ultimately
arrive late or even not at all, on account
of an unforeseen complication arising with
a patient? Of course, Duncan's job involved
the unpredictability of the human factor, so
that this was an unfair comparison, Frances
hastily reminded herself as she opened her
door to the arrival of Bernard's Citroën. He
got out and came forward to give her a hand
with her parcels.

'Writing paper and books,' she said, passing
over a plastic carrier which he stowed into
the boot. 'Home-made cake, the plans of the
new shop — oh, and these.' She retrieved an
armful of patterns and two bales of material
from the corner of the hall and came out on
to the step with them in her arms. Bernard
packed them away as she closed the front
door and locked it.

'You're looking very delectable,' he said,
holding the car door open for her. 'Is it
playing the game, showing the poor bugger
what he's missing?' His eyes swept over her
blue silk shirt, matching pleated skirt, calf

boots, and a blue mixtured scarf wound twice round her neck, its points resting on the top of her left breast. In the unbuttoned opening of her blouse lay a flat gold chain. His glance rested on it and Frances experienced a flicker of excitement low down in her stomach as she got into the passenger seat. 'I hope you didn't mind my suggesting coming with you,' he said, as he steered the car deftly between the pot-holes and emerged from Ullswater on to the main road.

'Not a bit. I welcomed it. These days aren't always easy.'

He shot her a glance. 'I imagine not.'

'It's getting harder to find subjects to talk about. I didn't realize before how much we discussed his work. Without that, there doesn't seem much to say. Depending on his mood, I tell him about mine. Today should be all right. I want to get him really interested in the building and the new designs. I've brought everything to show him, and if it goes well I hope to sow the seed of an idea Liz and I have got for his future. If he takes to it, it could be the turning point. He'd have a goal to work towards — one that would draw us closer together again.' She plucked at her skirt nervously. 'It's been frightening me how far things between us seem to have disintegrated.

113

One reads of disasters binding people to one another, but ours hasn't, though I have tried to be intelligent about it. I guess the growing fear is that the disaster happened long before this, only I wasn't aware of it. Somehow I've got to pull it all together.'

He made no comment except to ask, 'You want him to come into your business?'

'It's the obvious answer. We're going to need lots of new help, a whole reorganization. We're taking off, Bernard, in a big way. I was cautious at first, but I feel it in my bones that this extension is only the start. We'll need people to handle orders, accounts, advertising, and someone to administer those people while Liz and I are busy designing, making and selling. But he must be enthusiastic and in it heart and soul. We can't afford any passengers in the cause of rehabilitation. Do I sound tough?'

'You sound businesslike.'

She sighed. 'Just because it appears to offer the complete solution I mustn't take it for granted the idea is going to appeal to Duncan. He's got an outsize chip on his shoulder already about my dominant role, and being aware of that makes me less confident about making suggestions. You can lead a horse to the water — '

'Don't worry. This one will drink.' It was said with a sardonic certainty.

'Why do you say it like that?'

He let in the clutch and negotiated a narrow bend before answering. His face was set and concentrated on the road ahead. 'I know my animal. He'll kick against the pricks — indulge himself in some face-saving resentment that it's you he's got to thank — but he'll let you pick up the pieces.' He smiled, not very pleasantly, and Frances remembered Cambridge and David and who had picked up the pieces then. She was in no position to chide him for his sarcasm.

She said, 'It would have to be put to him tactfully. That's why I'm relying on you to help plug the idea. I've got a way of sounding bossy when I'm keen on something.'

He smiled again, but differently. 'I'd noticed.'

'I can't help it. I know it's unattractive. It had something to do with him going off with Ellen.'

Bernard turned to look at her. 'I don't find it all that unattractive,' he said. After that they drove in silence. The treasonable pleasure Frances gained from his compliment and the way in which it had been delivered warned her to beware of carrying discussion of Duncan's character further. The danger was

115

of being encouraged into an unintentional disloyalty of speech.

★ ★ ★

They stopped for lunch the other side of Petworth and for an hour Duncan wasn't mentioned. Bernard had chosen a village pub, inauspicious on the exterior, but inside displaying a menu of tempting hot dishes and a mouth-watering cold buffet. He had not asked for Frances's opinion, so she concluded the place was already known to him. She sat back in satisfaction at being so completely organized and taken in hand. They were seated on winged benches facing one another across their food, squashed into a corner, and there was no way of avoiding the contact of their knees beneath the narrow oak table. It would have been good to have been able to get up at the end of the meal and ride leisurely home after a pleasant day's outing, but with the coffee Frances remembered with a shock the purpose of their journey. It was a pity, she reflected an hour later, that they hadn't done just that, for Duncan was at his most depressed and self-pitying and she found his attitude more irritating than worrying.

He had been civil enough to Bernard,

who had remained with them for the first half-hour and had then made tactful excuses in order to leave them alone.

'As if we were honeymooners,' said Duncan morosely, watching his departing back. 'Fat chance of that here. Not that I suppose you're all that keen now.' He cast a sharp look at her. 'It doesn't seem to be affecting you too badly, Fran. You look blooming.' He made it sound like an indictment. Would he have preferred her to go into a decline, Frances wondered, but she preferred to ignore the remark and said lightly:

'I'm fine. Very busy. So much is happening. I want to show you how it looks now the builders are finishing at the shop.' She got out the plans and spread them before him. 'Now — this is the extra store, carried on here over the garage — the workroom here — extended by six feet, and this much wider.' She indicated the area. 'Liz's flat has been pushed out this way. She's got a proper studio for her drawing-boards and all her paraphernalia, which means we can use the room she had in the shop for an office. We'll need one now to house someone to do the accounts and shovel all the bumf. The bigger the business, the more red tape. We'll have to employ a man.'

'What are you using for money?' He

remained stolidly unimpressed.

'That's all taken care of. I've got a loan. The bank manager was very understanding. It's not as if we haven't got collateral and if things continue on the same lines it should be repaid over the next six or nine months.'

'Talking of money, I haven't heard of half these shares Bernard's bought for us — Amingos, South American Shipping — Midas Mining, Australia — Baxameter, China Clay,' said Duncan, changing the subject.

'Nor had I, but I'm learning. I have fun following their fortunes in the papers every day. I never had any interest in the stock market before, but now it's the first thing I look at when I open *The Times*. Does that surprise you?'

'It doesn't amaze me that you're obviously a damn sight better off without me and managing a great deal more competently.' His mouth twisted. 'Don't learn to do completely without me, Fran.'

She pressed his hand lying on the table between them. 'As if I could.' But as she said the words she knew it had been becoming easier to do so and it was this that worried her most. 'I've got the new batches of materials here.' She laid a swatch on top of the plans. 'These are for curtains. Tell me what you think. Would you put them with this?' She produced another sample and held the two patterns together.

'Does it matter what I think?'

'I'm asking for your opinion, Duncan. If you're not interested — '

'I can't stand being humoured.'

'Oh, for God's sake!' She attempted to control her exasperation. 'I'm trying to treat you like an adult. You could be invaluable to Liz and me if you took an interest in the business. There's a career there for all three of us — us and plenty more — if you got stuck in.' She had talked about broaching it subtly and now, in her usual fashion, she'd gone at it like a bull at a gate.

'I know nothing about interior decoration. It's a far cry from practising medicine,' he said sulkily.

'As you said yourself, so is peddling pharmaceuticals. That's the usual alternative, isn't it?' She was being abrasive to combat his defeatism and knew she sounded unsympathetic. 'I'm sorry. I didn't mean to be cruel. I've thrown the idea at you and not given you time to think about it. You may have other thoughts about the future. If you have, why don't you tell me?'

He laughed mirthlessly. 'I don't imagine they'll be queueing up to employ me. Apart from my record — what do I know about anything?'

Resisting the impulse to shake him, Frances said, 'This could be your opportunity to learn. Read up about a subject. Start a course. Take an exam. People do. Alternatively, I could start genning you up on the business. You could do some of the book work for us in here. Promise me you'll consider it.'

'I suppose most people would say I was lucky to be able to cash in on my wife's success.'

'No luckier than I to cash in on yours for many years,' Frances said quietly. With him in this self-flagellating mood it was hardly worth arguing, but she would never learn to give in. She changed the conversation. 'I saw your father the other day. He called in on his way down from town where he'd been making a speech at a posh lunch.'

'He hasn't been down here for a while.' Duncan frowned. 'Not that I enjoy him coming and seeing me here. Mother never comes. She writes.' They both thought about Amelia's letters.

'I wish they'd get rid of Falconers and move into something more manageable. Alistair said nothing, but I've a feeling there could be money worries. There's certainly something on his mind. He's aged a lot.'

'You can lay that at my door. Mother certainly will,' Duncan said bitterly. Frances sighed inwardly. All roads led back to Duncan and today they were all uphill. After another hour of it she was relieved when the bell rang for the end of visiting.

★ ★ ★

Bernard awaited her in the car. The day which had been warm and sunny had turned grey and heavy with the threat of thunder, and Frances's brain felt as leaden as the skies after the mental effort it had expended during the afternoon. Flopping into her seat she lay back, eyes closed, and drew in a couple of deep breaths.

'As bad as that?' Bernard threw his cigarette away and switched on the ignition.

She nodded. 'I wasn't much better. I try to be all sweetness and light and end up sounding harsh and unsympathetic, but honestly, Bernard, sympathy's not going to make him pull his finger out.'

'Don't talk about it now. Lie back and relax.'

She did as she was told. The upholstered comfort of the car, the sound of the engine and the cushioned springing of its motion combined to lull her into a gentle doze,

121

deepening to a sounder sleep, and it wasn't until they halted in a traffic jam somewhere near Chiswick that Frances awoke with a start and took stock of her surroundings. 'Where are we?'

'Nearly home.'

She peered out for identifying landmarks. It was raining quite heavily with the promise of settling into more than a shower. 'Whose home? We've overshot Richmond.'

'Mine,' he said blandly. 'I decided while you were asleep that you deserved a nice dinner to cheer you up, so I'm taking you home for that purpose. Any objections?'

She started to protest, then caught his eye and smiled. 'I can think of a million — all of them to do with work to be prepared for tomorrow, but I'm not going to make them.'

'Good.' They were still stationary and he put his hand across and patted her knee in the way that one would congratulate a dog or a child. 'We won't be long now.' The silk of her skirt slipped upwards and she felt his hand momentarily warm on her thigh. The innocent words coupled with the gesture assumed a pregnant promise, but she couldn't divine if that had been his intention as at that moment the traffic moved and all his attention was on driving.

Her common sense told her that she should have insisted on returning to No. 6, but her inclinations persuaded her it would have been unsophisticated and ungrateful to have done so.

The first clap of thunder exploded overhead as the Citroën nosed round three-quarters of Belgrave Square and turned into Brandon Court. They came to a halt in a residents' parking space opposite a row of whitewashed, porticoed houses facing some railinged gardens. Family residences in the days of horse-drawn carriages, they were now for the most part divided into offices on all floors. Bernard's was the exception. The ground floor of his building housed a publisher, the second, the offices of an estate agent, and on the third and part of the fourth Bernard's apartment enjoyed an uninterrupted view of the gardens, and a privacy afforded by a total absence of residential neighbours.

'There's only me and one other private owner at the end of the row left,' he explained when Frances commented upon the Court's Sunday air of desertion. 'Gradually all these places have been bought up by businesses. They did make me an offer but I'm not budging. Not until it suits me. I'm very comfortable here.'

They had made a dash to a smaller door

123

beside the main entrance under the porch, and he produced a key and opened it for her. Her shirt was heavily marked with the rain and as they stood there a flash of lightning forked down near enough the area railings to make Frances flinch.

'Go on in before you get any wetter,' he commanded, and pushed her through into a small hall in which there was a lift serving the second and third floors. Bernard closed the outer door, shutting them into a world of their own. The fact that she had shivered had nothing to do with her rain-spotted clothes.

# 9

Frances and Duncan had often in the past been entertained in Bernard's flat, but it was some time since she had been there and tonight she noticed he had made a number of changes. Before she took more than half a dozen steps into the hall of the apartment, he warned her not to go any further until he had de-activated the burglar alarm. A low buzzing that had commenced as he had unlocked and opened the front door, abruptly ceased as Bernard opened a wall cupboard near a flight of stairs and turned a key in a control panel fixed inside.

'Is this one of your innovations? Can I move now?' Frances asked nervously. 'I won't set anything off if I do, will I?'

'Quite safe now.'

She came up behind him and inspected the panel with its keyhole, two levers and three light bulbs. 'It looks complicated. Liz and I have been thinking we ought to have one of these things installed on our premises. How does it work?'

'It's really quite simple. The drawing-room, dining-room and kitchen doors into

125

this hall are all wired. If you'd opened any of those a siren would have gone off and an alarm bell goes straight through to the local police station. Likewise, the windows in the actual rooms — only they operate on rays. Anything crossing the ray path — say, someone putting their foot through the window — would do it. The same goes for upstairs. If you want to set it you turn these levers to the right, turn this small key in the panel, withdraw it, shut the cupboard door like so — ' the buzzing recommenced — 'that noise reminds you it's activated, then lock the front door.' The buzzing stopped. Bernard reversed the whole procedure and turned the alarm off. 'It's on two circuits so that when I go up to bed I can set this floor in case a prowler tries to get in at night. There are various permutations.'

'Very neat. And now that you've shown me exactly how it works, aren't you afraid I might come and do you over?'

He closed the cupboard and turned to stand quite close to her.

'Any time, Frances. It would be a pleasure.'

She laughed and moved ahead of him into the drawing-room. It was large, with a lofty ceiling and deep sash windows which looked towards Belgrave Square and ended in knee-high window-seats. At the far end of the room were some french windows leading out on to a fire-escape which disappeared down into a walled cutting between his house and the next. Bernard went round drawing heavy brocade curtains against the increasing storm and turning on the electric fire and a couple of table lamps. Meanwhile Frances noted his latest acquisitions. These included a number of pictures and ornaments that she did not recognize, and at least three pieces of mahogany furniture of the Victorian era were missing and had been replaced by others of an earlier and more valuable period. There were also the two new Persian rugs and a Baluchistan prayer mat.

On a marquetry table near the fire a chessboard was set out bearing ebony and ivory pieces, and between the two bay windows in the front stood an inlaid roll-top desk surmounted by a glass-fronted display cabinet. The ornaments inside were antique pieces of silver and china and the soft rosewood glowed mellow in the lamplight. Two deep chintz-covered couches ran out at right angles from the fireplace and there were three Victorian button-backed chairs, each upholstered in a single toning jewel colour, spaced about the room. To the right of the fireplace, between a tall narrow bookcase and the french window, the wall was hung with Bernard's pistol collection, the weapons arranged in a circular pattern, butts to the centre, barrels pointing outwards. He came over to her as she stood in front of them and ran his fingers lovingly over the chased silver mask butt cap of a flintlock pocket pistol.

'Exquisite workmanship, isn't it?'

'Is it very old?' Frances asked.

'Anything between 1790 to 1830. This one is 1750 — a flintlock duelling pistol.' He showed her the maker's name on the lockplate of a neighbouring gun. 'This is a pair of cannon barrel coach pistols. These are two percussion duelling pistols, *circa* 1850.'

'Are they worth a lot of money?'

'A fair amount. But I should hate to part with them.'

'This one looks out of place among those beautifully decorated ones.' Frances pointed to an ordinary black revolver at the base of the group. It was set on its own and looked ugly and lethal, whereas its companions were decorative enough to make one forget that they might have killed anyone.

'That's an Army issue Smith and Wesson, .38 calibre rimfire — a relic from the war. A number of people didn't hand them in after it was over. There must be a few lying about in attics and old gun-rooms all over the country, unaccounted for on any firearms certificate.'

'How did you come by it?'

'Alistair gave it to me.'

'Alistair?'

'I saw it a long time ago lying in a drawer at Falconers, when I was starting this collection, and fancied it. It too will be an antique one day.'

'And do you have to account for all of these?'

'Lord, yes. They all have to be listed on my certificate, plus any ammunition if one has it, which I haven't, so you needn't be afraid of me.' His eyes were shadowed, black and steely like the gun in his hand. Frances stepped past him over towards the fire. It was herself she was afraid of. He replaced the revolver on its peg. 'That's right, get warm and dry off a bit. I'm sorry — perhaps you'd like to titivate. You know the way. Go on up while I find something for us to eat.'

'Thank you. I think I will.'

He ushered her out into the hall and touched a light switch at the bottom of the stairs to illuminate what had once been an attic floor above. A spacious room under the eaves had been converted into Bernard's bedroom which, in turn, gave on to an elegantly appointed bathroom tiled in navy to match the porcelain fittings, and carpeted and papered in a light tobacco design. Frances did her hair and made up her face in the mirror over the basin, then washed her hands, drying them on a daintily embroidered guest towel put out for the purpose. Its presence suggested that all along Bernard had assumed she would return with him, but perhaps he was in the habit of preparing for unexpected visitors. Out of curiosity spawned by this thought, she opened the wall cabinet, searching for other clues, but there were none — certainly not of a feminine nature. The shelves were sparsely decorated with shaving tackle, toothpaste and a packet of aspirin and she was ashamed to be gladdened that it was so. His dressing-table was similarly uncluttered and the only ornaments in the bedroom were a Chinese lamp on the table beside the double brass bedstead and a softly lit French Impressionist painting above it. The storm was still rumbling around the rooftops and Frances could hear the force of the rain against the metal continuation of the fire-escape which ended outside this room beyond the window. She went across and pulled the curtains to shut out the lightning and the force of the gale.

Descending the stairs, she could see Bernard through the open kitchen door. Cutlery and china were assembled on a tray on the table, accompanied by wine glasses, a pepper mill and two plates of smoked salmon. A green salad tossed in french dressing and a jug of celery stood separately, and as Frances entered Bernard was deftly buttering and slicing a brown loaf and arranging the pieces on to a plate.

'Am I too late to help?'

'Just about ready.' He had removed his jacket and the sleeves of his shirt were rolled up over his forearms. Although Frances knew he enjoyed the reputation of being a more than competent cook, she had never previously been able to imagine him engaged in mundane domestic chores. 'If you like to take the greenery, I'll bring the tray and the bottle. We'll have it by the fire, shall we?' She followed him into the drawing-room where he laid the repast on a coffee table which he drew up to one of the couches. 'You come and sit here. There's cheese and fruit to come. Will that do?'

'Perfect.' Frances sat down where he had indicated nearest the fire, and he settled himself beside her, handing her the food and pouring wine into both their glasses. When they had finished eating he removed the tray and came back with a second bottle.

'You've thoroughly spoilt me today, Bernard, and I don't deserve it. I was fairly bloody to Duncan. I made a complete balls of suggesting he comes in with Liz and me. I'm far too impatient and I say things that hurt him. He's resentful, and I feel it growing in me when he's like that.' Frances sighed. 'It's self-destructive, but I can't help it. He's changed so.' Resting her head against the back of the sofa she turned it to seek from him some kind of an answer to her muddled thoughts.

He leaned across to top up her glass. 'Duncan's not changed. You said yourself, people don't. He's always needed a crutch, Fran. His father. Me. You. There'll always be someone. The question is, is it going to be you from here on in?' He put the query she had shied away from asking herself.

Before she could answer, they were diverted by a colossal clap of thunder that seemed to shake the whole house. A gust of wind blew the curtains inwards and there was a muffled crash as something over near the desk hit the carpet. They both stood up to see what damage had been done and Bernard hurried to the window to

132

pick up whatever it was that lay on the floor.

'Damn,' he said. 'I didn't pull the double glazing across and the draught came through. My fault for putting the thing on the window-seat. I must get a proper table for it. I've already been caught once with it setting off the alarm. Luckily I was here and was able to prevent the police hot-footing it here.'

'What is it?' Frances watched him lift the object carefully and inspect it for damage before replacing it.

'It's my new toy. An electrical mobile sculpture.'

She moved across to take a closer look. The thing — she could only describe it as that — had been assembled of glass and steel. It was a kind of pillar of jagged sea-green glass with fine steel arms of varying length extending from it. Depending from the arms, corrugated glass globules of differing sizes hung, bending the metal filaments in a downward arc. The whole was set on a round wooden base inset in which was a button switch and a flex which plugged into a socket on the skirting-board. Frances had not noticed it before as it had been obscured from view when Bernard drew the curtains.

'What does it do?' she asked.

'There speaks the practical Philistine. It's

133

a piece of art. Existing is enough.'

Frances eyed it dubiously. 'Not for me it isn't.'

'Well then, sit down again and all shall be revealed.'

She resumed her place on the couch, ready to be entertained as Bernard, with the air of a magician, went over to the door and flicked one of the wall switches, turning out the lamps. She heard him press down the adjacent one and by the light of the fire he made his way to sit down beside her. Gradually, in the dark, the glass pillar became suffused with an aquamarine light that slowly crept along its branches and into its faceted globules in waves of shaded green and blue. At the same time it began to rotate almost imperceptibly.

'It takes a bit of time to warm up,' said Bernard. 'From their lowest angle it takes twenty-five minutes to reach the point when all the arms are fully extended, then they decline and it starts again. I tend to forget to switch it off. That's what caught me out. It was on the window-seat and I left it on one day when I went up to get ready for bed. The longest tentacle went through the alarm ray across the window and set everything off.' The sculpture glowed like a ghostly emanation, disembodied in the gloom, and

Frances was forced to admit that in motion it possessed an ethereal modernistic beauty.

'What sort of a mind would dream that up?'

'A young artist I know. He has a studio in the Bayswater Road. He's going to make a reputation for himself in time. I invest in him from time to time when I can afford to.'

Frances's eyes had become accustomed to the shadows and she watched, fascinated, as the light on the glass created the optical illusion of changing shapes and texture.

'Anyway, where were we when that interruption occurred?' He held the wine bottle up against the firelight to gauge its contents, then refilled both their glasses. 'Ah yes. Duncan. How long are you going to prop him up, Fran?'

'As long as he'll let me, if that's what he needs. But you exaggerate his dependence on me. And I thought you were his friend and what you said just now about him didn't sound very friendly.'

'It's the truth.'

She said quietly, 'I know about Cambridge and what you did for him. He was very fortunate to have you there.'

'As he is to have you now. As he always will be. It's the weak that inherit the earth, Fran. More damage is done by their fumbling

135

inadequacies than can be assessed, and people like you and me go on making excuses for them and easing their path.' His face was tight with anger as he took a gulp of his drink, then swilled it round and finished it off.

'I didn't realize you still felt so bitter about it.'

'I'm not bitter for me. It's for you. You're wasted on him.'

'Don't say that.'

'I do say it. You're not made to be a wet nurse or a nanny for a boy who's never grown up emotionally. You were meant for a real man. Someone like me.' He covered the distance between them on the couch and took her face between the palms of his hands. His eyes were black and intense and only inches from her own. 'I've always wanted you — as you want me.'

Her body trembled with the excitement of knowing that soon his hands would move, and it could barely wait. She said simply, 'Yes.' The whole day had been a tantalizing crescendo building up to this moment, the whole time she had known him, possibly her whole life. Hypnotized by those eyes, she allowed him to draw her gently to her feet, then roughly against him. Liz had said nobody would blame her. Duncan had pleased himself with Ellen with no thought of her. She was entitled to take what she wanted for once. The future was uncertain. Even without these justifications, she had no will to turn back. He brought his lips down to hers and she slid a hand to the nape of his neck to increase their pressure, kissing him with a mounting ferocity equalling his own, opening her mouth and taking his questing tongue greedily into it, tasting, holding, drawing him in. His body was hard and demanding, lacking the timidity of Duncan's approach, not waiting for her gentle encouragement but forcing itself upon her consciousness. With one hand on her buttocks he pressed her against it now. With the other he undid the buttons of her shirt and put his hand inside to encounter the further restriction of her bra.

'Take them off,' he ordered hoarsely. He put her from him and while she did so, ripped off his own clothes, then came to her naked and intensely aroused. At the sight of him a hotter wave of erotic anticipation shot through her loins and breasts, and the urgent caress of his lips and tongue travelling from her erected nipples all the way down her body left her wet and shaking with desire. 'You're beautiful — beautiful.' He pushed her down on to the couch. 'I'm sorry Fran. I can't wait.'

Frantically close to the point of no return herself, she joyously assisted his violent entry and the world exploded and went mad. At the other side of the room the sculpture stretched and dipped.

★ ★ ★

Bernard lay in his brass bedstead watching slivers of daylight coming through cracks in the curtains and fingering their way across the ceiling. Soon he would have to waken Frances and speed her on her way. Before they had finally fallen into the stupor of exhaustion she had made him promise not to let her oversleep. She had to return to No. 6 to collect her requirements for a working day. He looked at his watch and decided to allow himself another half an hour in which to savour last night's turn of events, and then at Frances in the bed beside him. She lay on her side in a half-foetal position facing him, her head flung back on the pillow, knees drawn up, one arm curled under her, the other outstretched and resting across his body. His eyes followed the column of her throat down to her breasts, full and deeply cleft, the pink stains of their nipples spread in relaxation. Her stomach was flat and smooth, innocent of ugly stretch marks or operation

138

scars, the skin on her thighs soft and downy like a peach on the outside, silkily slippery within with the aftermath of his love. There was satisfaction in his gaze, not a little tenderness — and triumph. She had been worth waiting for and he had been patient for many years. He hadn't exaggerated when he had told her he had always wanted her. At their first meeting he had recognized a kindred spirit and a mutual sexual electricity, exciting enough in themselves, but made doubly so by the fact that she belonged to Duncan. Bernard smiled and stretched comfortably thinking of his friend. Duncan — by whom this world's plentiful supply of goods had been taken for granted; Duncan — who didn't know what it was to live on one's wits; who had proved convincingly he had none when it came to survival. He had been ripe for exploitation all those years ago when, as boys, they first encountered each other in a school locker-room.

Bernard had arrived at Harrow by courtesy of a scholarship, a defunct relative and the Church Commissioners, whose combined munificence covered the fees with nothing to spare for the provision of sports equipment, society subscriptions or pocket money necessary for outings or occasional entertainment. His father, staunch in the naïve belief that the Lord would provide, in his innocence overlooked the fact that the Almighty's provision for his own sparse needs bore little relation to the requirements of his son, thrust into the alien world of public school. In any case, among his father's mission, the calls upon what little money and energy he had were legion. Bernard was on his own and preferred to adopt the more practical adage that God helps those who help themselves. After a few weeks' careful reconnaissance he gravitated towards Duncan.

Duncan had been flattered. Brought up to accept conformity as original thought, Bernard's attitude to life was shockingly novel, his humour sophisticated and his brains undeniably sharper than most of his contemporaries. He was soon popular and regarded with some awe as being 'different', and his was an envied scalp on Duncan's belt. The latter had shown Bernard pictures of Falconers and spoken of his parents and their way of life, which seemed in no way extraordinary to him. He could not guess how well every prospect pleased his friend. Only the smallest degree of subtle angling had been necessary to secure Bernard's first invitation to Duncan's home. Once there, he had swiftly summed up the relationship of the parents with each other, and Amelia's with her son, and had decided that it would be tactical to go to work on the old girl. It had not been difficult to ingratiate himself with Amelia. His precocious flattery amused her and even in early puberty he possessed style, sadly lacking in Duncan. Bernard didn't bother so much about Alistair. Where Amelia led, he could be relied upon to follow. Yes, they had undoubtedly been generous throughout his boyhood. And then, just when they might have reasonably considered Bernard was capable of taking care of himself, Duncan had conveniently made the one false step that had ensured his friend's inclusion on Falconers' payroll for life. It had been neatly done, and it served them all right. The Parrys' capital wealth was inherited, not slogged for like the pittance for which Bernard's father sweated in some God-forsaken hole among savages and filth. Duncan might snivel about his mother's lack of warmth, but at the turning of a tap all material benefits flowed in his direction. Even Frances had fallen into his lap and he hadn't appreciated or known how to handle her. Poetic justice decreed that the spoils went to the strong. She was now securely in his, Bernard's, lap, and the turn of phrase made him randy again. He moved her sleeping hand further south and turned over to kiss her breasts.

Frances opened her eyes and drew him to her. 'What's the time?'

'Time for a quickie.'

'No. Seriously.' She twisted his wrist round so that she could read his watch dial. 'I must be going.'

'It's ten minutes fast.'

'Good.' She rolled over on her back and lay smiling up at him. 'I didn't know it could ever be like this.' The soft wonder shining in her blue eyes shamed him and he had a horrible feeling that she might be going to say she loved him. To forestall her, he covered her mouth and body with his own.

# 10

Frances had not meant to become totally committed to Bernard, but then neither had she intended falling passionately in love for the first time in her life. What had passed for that emotion in her relationship with Duncan, a one-sided satiation of his hunger for a mother figure and a degree of amiable tenderness, bore no similarity to the desire Bernard unleashed in her, or the uninhibited expression of her own personality he encouraged in her demonstration of that passion. With Duncan she had smothered eroticism and appetite, kidding herself that their love was the nobler for it. With Bernard no impulse need be stifled, so completely did her own match his. It was like suddenly running free after being fettered and she couldn't imagine willingly allowing herself to be re-chained. She postponed admitting as much to herself as the months passed by and she surrendered utterly to the intoxication of complete sexual compatibility. Their physical harmony served to underline and strengthen their already established mental union. Against her initial will, she had learned

143

to trust, rely on and respect Bernard, and he by his own admission admired her for the very strengths in her character that Duncan resented. They spoke the same language and laughed at the same absurdities, their minds grasshoppering to subjects without the liaison of explanations. Frances, in deep, didn't care if she never surfaced. A remnant of the instinct for self-preservation prohibited her from actually saying 'I love you' before he did. That he didn't, engendered no disappointment. Actions spoke louder than words, and when his actions fomented in her so delicious a delirium, where was the need for protestations of love? Giving her a key to his precious flat constituted an act of faith, if she were looking for one, and it was here that they met and made love at weekends.

Weekdays were complicated. With the enormously increased pressure of work at the business, Frances and Liz were working all the hours God sent, running late into most evenings and more often than not, right into the nights. When she finished at the shop, Frances was too tired to contemplate struggling up to Brandon Court and it would have been unwise to entertain Bernard overnight at No. 6. Tongues wagged and curtains twitched in Ullswater Road, and although Frances was on merely casual nodding terms with her neighbours, it was politic to guard against the possibility of any hint of gossip that might, for instance, be let slip in the hearing of a visiting inquisitive Dolly. As it was, no regular pattern on Saturdays and Sundays could be safely evolved. Suddenly absenting herself from No. 6 every weekend would inevitably call forth comment from Liz or Dolly, to whom her daily round was an open book. Fortnightly visiting Sundays were hers and Bernard's one sure bet, and Frances now found herself trembling in eager anticipation of her trips to Sussex, whereas before they had created only dread. Bernard would pick her up early, and they would meander through the countryside — sometimes picnicking, at others lunching in the same pub they had used — was it only six months ago? The day always ended with their return to his flat. Nobody expected her to be at home on visiting days and she and Bernard made the most of them. Once, unable to wait for the evening, he had taken her lying on a rug in a meadow with a stream running near by. She had been sure that her sensual gratification must communicate itself to Duncan as he later sat across the table from her, but he had noticed nothing different about her. Bernard seldom came in with her, but waited out of sight of the point where husband and wife bid one another goodbye.

On alternate Saturdays, Dolly had fallen into the habit of either expecting Frances to have supper with her, or to be invited to No. 6. Frances had wriggled on several occasions, for since Bernard, it had become even more imperative not to be trapped into an inflexible routine. The frustrations made their encounters increasingly intense and piquant, so that instead of waning, their desire burned brighter.

★ ★ ★

Bernard began to find himself hoist with his own petard. He had started the affair for his own gratification, as an erotic interlude to be terminated on Duncan's release. He had counted on Frances's highly developed sense of responsibility ensuring her continued support of her husband, and her principles prohibiting her bedding two men at the same time. Also, sooner or later, her opinion of himself would be affected by the knowledge of his misappropriation of the money Duncan had so trustingly insisted on handing into his care. Bernard might be able to stall Frances for a while, but inevitably the time would come when she and Duncan would want to cash in on the Trust fund and truth would out.

It had been childishly simple hoodwinking unsuspecting old George into approving Bernard's sole manipulation of the Trust. Having no reason to distrust his partner, and only too willing to absolve himself of extra business responsibilities as his career wound down towards retirement and total immersion in his outside interests, George obligingly and willingly put his name to whatever paper Bernard set before him. He was thankful that this was the limit of his charge in the matter. The list of shares with which Bernard had provided Frances was a tally of *bona fide* investments, ensuring the receipt of Company communications and dividend announcements. The amounts invested, however, falling ludicrously short of those quoted by Bernard to her, provided him with a useful residue to the tune of around £100,000 which he had converted to his own purposes. The quarterly cheques which he had delivered to Frances under the guise of investment income, had been for reasonable enough amounts to allay any possible suspicions, concealing the fact that nothing like the sum total of money entrusted to him had been invested. It had proved a lucrative operation and another example of his one-upmanship on Duncan.

Bernard had no fear of prosecution with discovery. He was confident enough that his hold over the Parrys would preclude so unpleasant a contingency. Until now it hadn't worried him that distaste would replace Frances's present love for him when she knew. Bernard would be rich enough for his own needs and have had a good run for his money. But now Frances had got under his skin and he didn't want to let her go. If he could convert her to his cause by an open confession combined with a declaration of love at the appropriate time, it was just possible that they might both enjoy jam tomorrow as well as today. There was a ruthless enough streak in her that might even applaud his panache if it coincided with her own inclinations. It would be a gamble, trying to make her see it his way, and tricky, but worth the attempt, Bernard decided. You could figure that half the money was rightfully hers anyway. The difficulty would be persuading her to ditch Duncan, having been a party to taking his as well. In normal circumstances Frances would never countenance anything fraudulent, but now she found herself in abnormal circumstances and he could tell she was beginning to wonder who she was. He was as much of a drug to her as she to him, and he must prevail upon that addiction to keep her for himself.

★ ★ ★

He started to put the pressure on.

'Time's running out. What are you going to do about Duncan?'

They had been to the prison that day and now lay in postcoital tranquillity in Bernard's bed. Duncan had been more animated than at any time since his sentence, with the prospect of a release date barely two months away. He had been more his old self and his behaviour had perversely provoked irritation in Frances. He had left it too late. Why hadn't he tried to remind her of this side of himself earlier when she had attempted in vain to muster her flagging loyalty? He had remained dogmatically resistant to the idea of slotting into a ready-made job with Frances and Liz in the firm. It was an expensive gesture of pride for which Frances found it harder still to respect him, but she had long since ceased to press her point. He had hinted at a nebulous plan of his own for the future but had not seemed willing to divulge any details, so she had held back from probing. Preoccupied as she was, it was becoming harder each time to summon interest in someone who had become a complete stranger. Their relationship had fallen apart but she was honest enough not to make that the excuse for her feelings for Bernard, who prodded her again with his question. She sighed. She didn't want to be made to think or to face reality at this moment.

'Have you considered?' He wasn't going to leave her alone.

She frowned. 'You know there's nothing to consider.'

'Isn't there?'

'How can there be?'

'You can leave him.'

She looked at him carefully. 'And?' Two could play the forcing game.

'And throw in your lot with me.'

He had surprised her. She hadn't expected anything so straightforward. 'Is that what you really want?'

'Yes.' He'd made up his mind.

'You've never said so before,' she said, after a pause.

'I wasn't sure before.'

She reached up and kissed him lightly on the lips. 'Thank you for the compliment — even if the reason you're sure now is that you know it's impossible.'

'Why is it impossible?'

'You know very well I couldn't live with myself if I deserted him at this point.'

It was irritating not to be taken seriously now that he was in earnest.

'So we're to be sacrificed to your ego?'

'He'll need me — then more than before.'

Bernard sighed exasperatedly. 'The eternal cry! Isn't it the truth, Fran, that you're flattered by that need?'

'You admit he has to have props,' she said indignantly.

'You might be doing him more of a service letting him stand on his own feet.'

'You didn't when he needed you. Was that an ego trip too?'

She had him there. If she knew what kind of a trip it had really been! More of a ride, really. A ride to the cleaners! There were a lot of things she would eventually have to know.

He persisted. 'There just comes a time when you have to look to your own happiness. If you tell me yours is Duncan. Fran, I simply won't believe you. Not after us. You should have married me in the first place. We're two of a kind.'

She looked at him and saw that he was sincere. 'You really do mean it.' She shook her head. 'There are too many complications, even if I could do it to Duncan — there's his father, for one.'

'For Christ's sake, Fran, stop leading everyone else's lives.'

'One does have responsibilities.'

'You sound like a schoolmarm. They're grown men. Duncan's had more chances than most. Alistair's done all right and anyway, his life's running down. People have to be responsible to and for themselves. Those two have had more material advantages than you or I started with.' He caught her looking at him strangely. 'What's the matter?'

'That bugs you, doesn't it?' she said slowly. 'You're really jealous.'

'I used to be,' he admitted.

'That's funny. I remember I asked Duncan once if he were jealous of you. It seemed to me he had cause. I suppose I recognized then that you were everything he wasn't, as well as having the admiration of his mother — something he wanted so badly.'

'What do *you* want, Fran?' He looked searchingly into her face with an intensity that made her realize this wasn't just an ordinary conversation. 'You *must* decide. Forget about nobility and playing God. You have a right to take what you want for yourself in this life. Most people do it all the time. You're a late starter, but I could teach you.'

'You have already. I can't go back, but — ' She felt as if she were beginning to drown.

'No buts. None of that crap about not living with your conscience, either. Strip off all the conditioning. What do you want?'

She shivered, and as her skin contracted she had the strangest fancy that it was being sloughed off with a lifetime's concepts of behaviour and an image of herself hitherto preserved for others. The Frances they had known had been a woman only half alive. For their sakes, was she bound to preserve that woman to the denial of the real Frances's fulfilment? People got hurt whatever one did, and no actions of hers could keep them safe for ever. It would have been different if there had been children at stake.

'I want you,' she said.

'Always? No matter what?'

'Warts and all. I want you.'

He still held off. 'Don't joke about the warts. There are some you don't know about. You might not like them.'

She smiled. 'Show me where. I'll charm them away.' Taking his hand, she laid it on her breast. 'You haven't said you want me — always, no matter what.'

She was totally shaken when he unexpectedly

153

laid his lips against hers and she caught his words. 'I think I love you.'

★ ★ ★

She felt as though she was travelling in a boat fast approaching the rapids. The current compelled her along its only course and the scenery left behind no longer held any enchantment. She had made up her mind. Bernard had said he loved her. Because the words had not been produced glibly before, they had been the deciding factor. It was now a matter of how and when best to tell Duncan, and over this she procrastinated until Bernard threatened to do it for her.

'The longer you wait, the worse it will be.'

She knew it was true but she searched vainly for a way to soften the blow. Four weeks passed and it was in the middle of her dilemma that she received a phone call from Alistair. He rang her at the shop, so she knew whatever was on his mind must be important as his normal rule was to call from home in the evening during the cheap rates. After an exchange of pleasantries, he said he was in town, would be travelling down to Falconers that evening and could he stop off at No. 6 to discuss some business with her.

It was immensely relaxing to sit in Alistair's kind and caring presence once more, and if he hadn't been Duncan's father, it would have been comforting to have thrown herself upon his understanding. He might be disappointed in her, but Frances prayed that the affection between them was too strong to be completely obliterated by her proposed course of action.

'I've had a couple of letters from Duncan — three over the past month, and also today a phone call.' He searched his pockets and produced the missives. 'He asked me to look into the possibility of buying up a small publishing house that's for sale Basingstoke way. Apparently he's got very friendly with a chap called Guy Ainsley who's in that place with him. This fellow's a journalist by profession and done some editing. He and Duncan have dreamed up the idea of going in together producing medical catalogues, pharmacopoeia, home medical care books, first aid — that type of thing. An erstwhile colleague of Guy's is selling this business. That's how he got to hear of it.' Seeing Frances's blank expression he said, 'You knew nothing of this?'

She shook her head. 'He mentioned an idea in the air — but no details. Go on.'

Alistair cleared his throat. 'Well, I've been

155

down there, looked over the place. It would seem to be a reasonable sort of proposition, but it would require a considerable sum of money to take over and start up.'

'How much?'

'My guess is nearer two hundred thousand than one, from estimates I've seen and going into it fairly thoroughly with my accountant.'

'But that would take more than we've got — apart from my business.'

'Exactly. And you've still got to buy a house and have something to live on when he comes out. That's what I told him.'

Frances was silent. She was thinking that even without her, Duncan would need accommodation of some sort, but he would also be better off financially than his present calculations if they were divorced. As a childless woman with an income from her own business, she would be unlikely to get maintenance or even a half share of his goods — not that she would ask for either in the circumstances. Bernard would classify her as insane but it would go a small way to appeasing her conscience.

'I wish he had told me,' she said. 'He didn't even say anything to Bernard who handles our finances.'

'He wanted to do this off his own bat. He

knew you thought him unreasonable turning down your offer of work, and hoped to show you he could fend for himself. He was afraid you'd insist on sacrificing yourself if the money could be scraped together. Telling Bernard would mean you might know. He wanted an independent assessment — so he asked me.'

'I see.' Once more Duncan had cast her in the role of martyr and blamed her for it. 'What about this Guy Ainsley? What's his contribution?'

'Not much money, but all the expertise, according to Duncan.' Alistair saw her tight, set expression. 'I told him it wasn't a flier financially — that is, until today.'

'Oh? What's changed today?'

'Duncan says you've got shares in Midas Mining. You haven't seen the paper?'

'Only the headlines. The same yesterday. I generally see the share prices but — what are you trying to tell me?'

'They've made a killing. Apparently they've found another two seams out there. Duncan read it and rang me to hold his options open on the publishers. He was allowed one phone call, so he asked me to put you in the picture — and Bernard. How much have you got invested in them, Fran? Do you know?'

'Just a minute.' Feeling dazed, Frances

157

went to the desk and found the list Bernard had given her. 'Midas,' she read. 'Five thousand shares bought at eighty pence a share. What are they now?' she asked Alistair. 'The paper's over there.'

He opened it and spread it on the table. Excitedly they both ran their eyes down the columns, each wanting to be first with the confirmation of the good news. 'Here it is. Midas — up to £12.' He looked at her triumphantly.

'That means ours are now worth £60,000!' she said incredulously. 'From £4000 to £60,000 overnight. I don't believe it. It also brings this scheme of Duncan's within the realms of possibility,' she said more soberly.

'That's what he figured. It would give you both the leeway you'll need.'

'Yes.' She stood lost in thought. The money represented freedom for both of them. The devil certainly looked after his own!

'Not many wives would be as unselfish as to risk this, plus all they've got, to give their husbands a new start, Fran. You know how I appreciate all you've done,' Alistair said awkwardly. 'How you've stuck by Duncan. Amelia does too, in her heart.'

The pressure of his compassionate hand on her arm made her feel cheap, and she

158

moved away involuntarily. 'Don't say that.' She could see that she had wounded him by her withdrawal and suddenly found that she couldn't insult him with further dishonesty. 'Don't count on me.'

During a pause, the words sank in, then he asked, 'Personally, or for Duncan?'

She drew a deep breath. 'For him.'

He nodded, accepting the fact. 'You've had enough. I suppose I can't blame you.'

'It's not just that. There never was 'enough' between us. I know that now.'

His face was sad and drawn with the acquiescence of one hearing expected bad news. 'To have learned that means you have fallen in love with someone else.'

'Yes.' His perspicacity clearly astonished her.

He nodded again at the endorsement of his own thoughts. 'You'll tell Duncan?'

'Yes, I must. But after we get this tied up. I shan't need any of his money. I feel very badly about him, but what you've told me and then this stroke of luck makes me feel less guilty. He may even be better without me. I sometimes feel I'm not as much help to him as I mean to be. Will you get on to Bernard about the shares, or shall I?'

He hesitated. 'Better you take it from here,' he decided. 'Releasing say £40,000 would show these people the colour of Duncan's money and clinch the deal. In his circumstances they may need reassuring. There'll be a number of expenses.'

'When will you let them know?'

'I'll alert them first thing tomorrow morning — Tuesday. Perhaps you could ring and give me a progress report on Friday.'

'Right.' She stood irresolute, then made a gesture. 'Alistair, I'm so sorry.'

His eyes were moist but he managed a rueful smile. 'One can only take so much.' She was uncertain whether he referred to her predicament or his own. 'There's definitely a limit. Frances, I'm too fond of you to see you get hurt any more. This man, whoever he is, will he take care of you?'

'I believe so.' She found it impossible to rub salt into the wound by revealing his identity at this moment.

'It will be a severe blow to Amelia.' His face creased in pain. She was his first consideration — before his son's possible reaction to Frances's desertion.

'Will it?'

The irony was not lost on him. Alistair defended his wife. 'She may not have shown you her best side at times, Frances, but she recognizes you've been good for Duncan. She finds it difficult to be demonstrative.'

Frances grimaced. 'You make me sound like castor oil.'

'More of a splint. You strengthened his backbone.'

'A crutch,' she amended, more to herself than to him.

'It's my failure that he has need of a cripple's aid.'

'No.' She couldn't allow him to shoulder Amelia's blame. It was painful enough to hear his admission of Duncan's short-comings.

'Don't blame his mother too much, Frances.'

Her heart twisted for him. 'I should be lucky to be loved by someone as much as she is loved by you.' His tolerance and understanding humbled her. She embraced him, managing to hold back her own tears to shed in private after his departure.

# 11

After Alistair had left her, Frances tried phoning Bernard at the flat with no success, so had to be content with waiting until the next morning and ringing him before she left for work.

'You've caught me at a bad time, Fran. I'm going to Manchester for a day or two and I'm packing a suitcase. I was going to ring you when I got there. Something came up unexpectedly yesterday. I'll be back for the weekend.' He sounded harassed.

'I won't keep you then, darling, but this is rather important. Are you up to date with what's been happening to our Midas shares?' There was a sudden stillness at the end of the line and Frances said 'Hullo' again to see if he had been cut off.

The second time he answered. 'Yes, I'm here. What about them?'

'Our £4000 investment has turned into £60,000 in the past two days, that's what. Isn't that incredible! I want you to sell £40,000 worth for me.' Another silence communicated itself. 'Bernard!'

His voice sounded muffled when it came.

'It's a bad line, Fran. I can't do anything about this till I come back. We'll talk then.'

'That won't do,' she insisted. 'It's urgent. I've got to know about the money by Friday. It's for Duncan.'

'What's he doing — planning a break? Come on, Fran, if it's for Duncan, there can't be that much of a hurry.'

'It's for a business he wants to buy. Look, sweetie, it's a long and complicated story and you're in a hurry. I'll fill you in later, but Alistair's vetted the whole proposition and he needs the cash Friday at best, Monday latest.'

He stalled. 'These things take time to arrange. It's not like cashing a cheque at the bank. Besides, I'm not going in to the office this morning.'

'Ring George then. He's co-trustee. Ask him to get things moving.'

'Frances, are you sure all this is a good idea? It sounds to me rushed and not sufficiently considered. What has Alistair got to do with it? How can Duncan buy a business he's never seen?'

Frances was getting impatient. 'I told you — there's a whole lot more to it and all kinds of reasons. Duncan and this friend of his have apparently got it all worked out.

163

Alistair's been into it too. Bernard! It would get Duncan off our necks as well.'

He was less impressed by the appeal of this aspect than she had expected. 'Does he really know what he's doing? There's Capital Gains and God knows what involved. There's no need to go mad just because the shares have jumped up. If what you say is true they'll probably go further — certainly won't slump before Friday.'

In spite of herself, her voice dropped an iced semi-tone. 'Bernard, it's his money. Will you please do as he asks?'

He realized he couldn't hold her off any further at present and made placatory noises. 'All right, all right, Fran. Thy will be done! I'll give George a ring. I just hope you all know what you're doing. I'll be back around six Saturday evening. Come to the flat and we'll do some filling in then.' He made the last sentence sound like a lewd promise and they both laughed at the *double entendre*.

'I'll keep you to that,' she said softly. 'I shall be empty till then. Dolly's pinned me down to supper at eightish, but we could have an hour and a half before that.'

'And Sunday!'

'And Sunday.'

Bernard put the phone down feeling as if someone had punched him in the stomach.

He had known he was going to have to bullshit himself out of this one with Frances at some point in time, but had counted on the revelation being deferred until she had actually left Duncan and his own hold upon her was more permanent. The option was to sell up and disappear without her, but quite apart from the time factor, this he was reluctant to do. No doubt he was mad, but he wanted Frances, and he wouldn't give up without trying everything he knew to keep her. He had an hour and a half on Saturday to persuade her. Until then he could do nothing but sweat.

★ ★ ★

Bernard didn't contact Frances from Manchester, but she wasn't unduly worried, deducing that business or the entertaining of clients had made it difficult for him to be near a phone at a convenient time. She had been disciplined not to ring Duncan at the hospital or surgery and wouldn't have dreamed of interfering with Bernard's working commitments, even had she known his number. Frances scorned wives who rang their husbands' offices on trivialities, making the men look as if they were tied to their apron strings, and in any case that week she was more than occupied herself.

Alistair phoned on Tuesday evening to say that the people in Basingstoke were interested that Duncan was still in the market, and Frances was able to tell him that Bernard was attending to the sale of the shares.

'He hummed and hawed a bit,' she told Alistair. 'Thought you and Duncan were being a bit precipitate. Was afraid you might get your feet wet, but he was only being cautious. You are sure this idea is sound, aren't you, Alistair?'

'Why don't you come and see for yourself? We could go down there together. Say Thursday. It might be a good thing for the vendors to see you. Give them a feeling of security, and you can satisfy yourself.'

'Duncan might think I'm interfering.'

'I should value your opinion, Frances.'

She capitulated.

Once there, Frances's critical business eye saw immediately the advantages and potential of the scheme. She was secretly astonished at the detailed grasp of the project shown by Duncan and the as yet unknown Guy Ainsley, and could only conjecture that the latter was the driving force. The driving force on Duncan's money perhaps, but many excellent partnerships had been founded on a similar basis. The reassurance that Alistair's years of commercial experience backed Duncan's own enthusiasm on this occasion satisfied her that the reason she believed this venture could succeed was not purely selfish.

'I'm so glad you took me down there,' she said to Alistair on the way home. 'I know it's not going to be any concern of mine, but it makes me feel better knowing what he's coming out to. I'll be able to set Bernard's mind at rest too. Not that Duncan has to justify himself selling shares, but you'd have thought it was Bernard's own money I was asking him to shell out the other morning. Mind you, I caught him on the hop. He was on the point of departure and the line was bad. It's probably my imagination that he was looking for all kinds of difficulties.'

Alistair, who was driving, carefully changed down behind a lorry crawling up a steep gradient and flexed his gloved hands on the steering-wheel, curbing his impatience to pass. 'To my mind, it's a pity Duncan gave Bernard control of the money at all.'

'Oh? You didn't say so at the time.' Frances was surprised.

'There wasn't any time. You told me how it was done. Even you had no say. If you remember, I did try to warn you and to offer my services once.'

'Warn me?'

He didn't answer and the noise and fumes from the lorry ahead penetrated the car and made Frances's head feel thick and her senses stupefied. 'Not about Bernard? Why should you warn me about Bernard?'

He still said nothing, his silence increasingly pregnant.

'Alistair! What are you trying to say?'

He spoke at last. 'Nothing. I can't.' He turned his head and looked significantly into her dismayed eyes.

'You don't trust him,' she said slowly and unbelievingly. 'You don't even like him.' The wonder in her voice demonstrated that this was a completely new idea to her. 'I don't understand. You've done everything to encourage him. Treated him like a son. Amelia adores him.'

'That's right.' He drove steadily on.

Frances got annoyed. 'Well, you can't just throw in a casual spanner like that and not elaborate. If you're accusing Bernard of something, come out with it. I ought to know.'

They were at the top of the hill and had accelerated, leaving the juggernaut behind, and with a clear road ahead. Alistair, avoiding her searching and puzzled glance, shook his head. 'Nobody's accusing anyone. I'm sure there was no reason for Bernard to stall you on the shares. Did you say something about a departure? Where was he going? Had he decided to leave before or after you asked about the money?'

'My God!' She sat beside him, stunned. 'I don't believe it. You don't seriously mean you think Bernard is a crook? Is that what you're telling me?'

'Business teaches one to have a nasty suspicious mind.'

Annoyance was turning to anger. He must have flipped completely to be suggesting such a thing. Perhaps he wanted to get his own back on her for what she had told him earlier in the week. She said icily, 'He was packing for Manchester when I rang.' That's what Bernard had said. She had no proof. The Judas worm of doubt wriggled. 'Are you suggesting the money's not there? It's really too absurd.' Did he somehow know that it was Bernard who was her lover and was deliberately attempting to put her off?

'I hope it is. I'm sure it is,' he added hastily as if afraid he had gone too far in giving her the wrong impression. 'But you should be more wary, Frances.'

'If I'd been more wary I'd never have married your son,' she said furiously and hurtfully. She was totally bewildered. In spite of herself, his words had awoken reluctant suspicion, coming shockingly as they did from one whose judgement she valued as fair. Allied to these were snatches of incidents, vague sensations, fleeting intangibles that assailed her memory. The coolness she had perceived between the two men on meeting outside the Magistrate's court that morning months ago, Bernard's attitude when she had suggested he visit Falconers more often, her own unaccountable disquiet on being forced to sign the Trust paper, Liz's half-joking doubt of Bernard's integrity — above all, the very definite impression gained during their recent telephone conversation that Bernard had been temporarily thrown by her unexpected request for the Midas sale. At the time she had attributed his slow response to a poor connection and his protestations to responsible concern, but now — she scarcely knew what to think. Set against her private knowledge of Bernard and their love, she told herself it was all ridiculous, and yet what possible axe could Alistair have to grind by planting malicious doubts in her mind? He had made no actual allegations, but it wasn't in his nature to stir up trouble purely mischievously.

He had chosen to ignore her small outburst, but a cord of sinew in the slack flesh of his neck pulled tight as his chin trembled. A dew drop rested under his nose on his moustache and he took out a handkerchief and wiped it away. Frances's anger evaporated. There was a dull apprehension in her stomach as she repeated quietly, 'Is there something I ought to know?'

'There's nothing I can tell you, my dear.'

'He's coming back on Saturday evening at six,' she said, as if stating the actual time vindicated her belief in Bernard. There were two days and two nights to be got through before she saw him. A thought slid into her mind so readily and swiftly that she was ashamed at the ease with which it had come. In the interim, a solution for satisfying any qualms raised by the present conversation lay conveniently to hand. What more natural in Bernard's absence than that she approach George Bruton for news of the share deal? It wasn't a question of checking up on anyone. She would require the information tomorrow. Bernard had known that.

Frances spent the rest of the drive in an agony of self-justification. The laws of social intercourse prescribed that she and Alistair engage in a stilted parody of normal discourse until he dropped her at the door of No. 6 and it was a relief to be safely inside, alone and punch-drunk with a series of chaotic thoughts.

In the morning, the little that Alistair had said seemed rather less significant than it had done at the time. Frances told herself she had over-reacted to an old man's emotional anxiety on her behalf and read into his concern all nature of evil omens. His warning had not been against Bernard in particular. It was true Alistair had made the suggestion that he might be absconding for good, or some such rubbish, but in the clear light of breakfast-time Frances couldn't even be sure of that. Inhaling the exhaust fumes from that lorry had fuddled her brain. Alistair hadn't looked well for a long time. She had been the first to notice the fact. Elderly people got bees in their bonnets and likes and dislikes became magnified and distorted.

If all this were so, it was not easy to account for the sick misgiving with which Frances presented herself at the offices of Bruton and King the next day. Having conceived the notion of pumping George, instinct had urged her to pursue it immediately, and taking a decisive course of action was, with her, always preferable to remaining a prey to doubts, however absurd.

'Mrs Parry. What a delightful surprise. When you rang this morning, that's what

I said to myself. A really delightful surprise to see Mrs Parry. Some coffee?' George had divested her of her coat and, all amiability, offered her his own swivel chair as he stood and beamed down at her. Frances declined the coffee, anxious to press on to matters of substance, but to George Bruton, coarse money topics had, of necessity, to be introduced with sweeteners like discussion of the weather, the church fête and the Conservative sponsored walk, so that by the time he came around to 'And now, Mrs Parry, in Mr King's absence, what can I do for you?' Frances's palms were sweating.

'I gave Mr King some instructions about selling some of my husband's shares,' she began. 'I believe he asked you to deal with the matter and I wondered what had been the outcome as my husband has a purpose for the money and needs it immediately.'

'Ah yes. And when would that have been, Mrs Parry?'

'I spoke to Mr King on Tuesday morning — just before he left for Manchester.'

'Manchester. Yes.' George mused benignly while Frances longed to put a boot behind him.

'Have you sold them?'

'Myself? Certainly not. Mr King alone attends to your Trust fund, Mrs Parry. You know that. Such great friends.'

'But he instructed you to make this transaction?'

George shook his head, still smiling as though humouring a child.

'There must be some mistake.'

Frances's heart commenced a slow descent. 'He didn't ring you on Tuesday morning?'

'No.'

'You would remember?'

'Dear me, yes. No call has come through from Mr King since I saw him on Monday.'

'None of your juniors could have failed to pass on a message?'

'Extremely unlikely, but I will check with them if you wish.'

'No, no, that's all right. It's not that important.' Frances didn't want to invest the incident with too much importance. There would be a perfectly reasonable explanation, she was sure, once Bernard got back, and it would be difficult to explain any reported over-anxiety on her part. She rose, as if to leave, then carefully hesitated half-way to the door.

'I'll be seeing Mr King next week in any case. Perhaps, while I'm here, I could just look at the share certificates to refresh my memory on exactly what the situation is.'

Momentarily George Bruton's sunny

expression clouded, then cleared.

'Mr King doesn't usually like me interfering with the papers of his private clients, but I'm sure in your case — excuse me.' He rose and went over to a filing cabinet by the window and, unlocking it, fished in the depths of its interior, retrieving triumphantly a bunch of keys. Selecting one from the ring, he used it to open an antiquated-looking safe which stood in a recess behind his desk. 'Here we are.' Withdrawing a pile of buff-coloured folders, he sifted through them until he came to one marked 'Parry' in bold capitals written with a felt pen. He handed it to Frances. The telephone on the desk rang and George leaned across and lifted the receiver. There was a brief conversation composed of 'yes' and 'no', two grunts and a nod, then 'All right, I'll come down.' Replacing the instrument, he addressed himself to Frances apologetically.

'Will you excuse me a moment, Mrs Parry? A slight altercation in the other office over a matter that needs my attention. I'll be back with you in two shakes.'

'Of course.' She watched him return the other folders to the safe and waited for him to leave the room before opening her own. Inside, on top, lay a thin sheaf of correspondence — stock letters with the

175

headings of Baxameter, Amingos, Midas and a couple of other companies, confirming the purchase of shares. She picked out the Midas ones, attached to carbon copies of Bernard's own letters, and read them through twice before turning to the back of the folder to find the share certificates referred to in them.

It was very quiet in the office — double-glazed against the traffic noise outside, and it was some moments before Frances realized that the drumming in her ears and head was the sound of her own accelerated pulse rate, a repetitive voice in her brain kept telling her that she shouldn't have been surprised. Why had her intuition guided her here if she hadn't expected to find a discrepancy once Alistair's seed of doubt had been sown? It was the open effrontery and careless bravado in the way Bernard had left the file open for everyone to see, should they so wish, that astonished her. No doubt he had figured that concealment of it would have excited more curiosity than including it among the rest. He had counted on George complaisantly leaving the Parry file to him, signing documents without necessarily reading them through, unaware of the amount that should have been invested. The likelihood of Frances herself asking to see the correspondence or certificates was remote, trusting Bernard implicitly as he had taken pains to ensure that she should, and Duncan was safely tucked away where he couldn't be inquisitive. There was no time now to dwell upon the psychology of any of their positions. That was for later. She had come seeking facts and she must note them down for accurate reference.

As one anaesthetized, she took a ballpoint from her bag and started making notes on the back of an envelope she also found there. The sum total of shares bought among the companies amounted to a derisory five or six hundred, accounting at purchase for £1500 at the outside. No evidence of any other investment existed in this file, and Frances's spirits rose fractionally on the hope that perhaps George had inadvertently provided her with only half the evidence. There must be another folder — one he probably knew nothing about, concerning Premium Bonds, National Savings, all the other carefully worked out safeguards for their money that Bernard had so plausibly suggested. She remembered he had given her the list of shares purported to have been purchased soon after the cheque from Hill House had been handed over. According to that, they had been acquired in bulk blocks at one time, not accumulated over a period. Frances consulted the buying dates of the certificates in the folder. Without exception they tallied with the month in which the house had been sold and shortly before Bernard had made out the list. Certainly, as far as the shares were concerned, her faintly revived hopes now faded. Accepting that Bernard had lied about those, only a fool would still cling to the belief in the existence of the other promised securities. It was an apt enough description of herself and Duncan. Fools both. Naïve and trusting utter bloody fools! If only she had listened to her instinct and refused to sign away her control of their finances. Duncan had ever been gullible where Bernard was concerned. If she had stuck to her earliest premonitions — if she hadn't been so fearful of emasculating Duncan — if she had resisted the physical attraction always at the heart of her friendship with Bernard — if — if — if! If she hadn't bloody well fallen in love with him! Even sitting in George Bruton's office with most of her suspicions confirmed, Frances was unable to regret completely that one fact. Anger kept the pain at bay — anger and the need for caution. She had twenty-four hours in which to decide how to play this new ball game. There was no profit yet in alerting Bernard's partner.

When George returned she was standing by the window looking out, the folder closed upon the desk.

'I'm sorry, Mrs Parry. Have you had time to find out what you wanted to know?'

She turned, composed and smiling. 'More than enough, thank you.'

'If there's anything that needs explaining, I'm at your service.' He flipped the file open, anxious to be of help.

'No, nothing thank you. Except — that is the whole record, isn't it? There are no other files or any other documents I should see?'

'No. Everything should be there.'

'Mr King doesn't keep any certificates in the bank — bonds and the like?'

'No. I assure you, Mrs Parry, everything is quite safe and most confidentially kept here.'

'I'm confident it is.' They shook hands and parted, George having accompanied her to the street door.

★ ★ ★

Standing on the pavement, she knew she ought to go back to the shop where there was work waiting for her. She had left Liz to carry the can yesterday when she had

179

gone off with Alistair. He was going to phone tonight and she had no idea what she was going to tell him. There wasn't any money for Duncan's venture. Come to that, there wasn't any money — period. She had her own business but how could she leave him penniless and without a job when he came out of prison in three weeks' time? Staring sightlessly at the plane trees across the street, she wondered dully if Bernard did intend to return or if, as Alistair had inferred, he might have opted out for good. It was a clumsy sort of a fraud. He must have known he would have been found out. £100,000 or thereabouts didn't seem enough to jeopardize everything for, but perhaps they hadn't been the only suckers on Bernard's list. It salvaged a little of her pride to think there might have been others — that what he had done to them, to her, had been less personally calculated. There were too many confusing aspects to be considered in detail here. She must go home.

Frances looked about her as if realizing for the first time where she was. Everything in the world had shifted and changed, like a kaleidoscope slipping into a new and unrelated pattern at a turn of the lens. Some of the edges were jagged. The only constant factor was the fierce ache in her heart which reminded her that she loved and wanted Bernard irrespective of what he might have done. She started walking towards where she had left the car.

# 12

After dinner on Friday evening Alistair excused himself to Amelia and went into his study on the pretext of having some letters to write. The depression that had settled on him during the past week, deeper than its regularly recurring predecessors over the years, weighed on his tired spirit, presaging the breaking-point he had successfully staved off innumerable times before.

It had begun with Frances's declaration of her intention to leave Duncan and intensified during the time since their abortive conversation in the car. He could have saved them all from so much unhappiness if he had been a man in the first instance, but from one original act of cowardice, compounded of necessity by others since, he had, with the best intentions, paved a road to hell for all of them. All of them except Amelia. He comforted himself with that thought. He had achieved his aim of shielding her from extra disillusion. Her dreams had been satisfied in his success and their position. He had promised her both when he had asked to marry her, and hadn't believed his luck when she had accepted him in his obscurity. Dazzled and enchanted by an imperious charm which in youth, mixed attractively with innocence, concealed the strength of her resolve, he was determined to live up to her. He had seen through a glass brightly, and even the face-to-face vision in forty years of marriage had not dimmed his adoration. Alistair had been as earnest for Duncan to please her as the boy himself, and he found himself acting as buffer between mother and son, excusing Duncan's actions to her and extolling Amelia's standards to him. Amelia was not overly maternal. One child was enough of an interruption of her relationship with her husband, so the onus to be creditable was on Duncan alone. Alistair's mistake had been over-compensation in sheltering him.

And then Duncan had brought Bernard home. Alistair had distrusted him on sight. The boy had treated him with a politely veiled contempt in his own house, reserving his bumsucking technique for Amelia who was impressed and sympathetic to his homeless status. Besides, he kept Duncan out of the way. 'We must help him,' she told Alistair when he demurred at the complete encroachment of Bernard into their family life. 'There's nowhere else he can go.' Alistair kept the opinion that Bernard would always land butter side up strictly to himself. It was ridiculous to be jealous of the attention Amelia paid him and her pride in him, but Alistair was — on his own behalf and for Duncan. At the same time he watched with concealed disquiet the degree of uncritical admiration and affection Duncan lavished upon his friend. 'Unhealthy' was an adjective Alistair hesitated to use openly, but it had intruded into his mind. When, therefore, Bernard had seen fit to apprise him of the details of Duncan's homosexual affair at Cambridge, the physical fact came as less of a surprise than that the object of his son's affection was someone other than Bernard himself.

Alistair could recall every detail of that interview. It had taken place in the study in which he now sat, and in spite of their difference in years, Bernard had been in command all the way. He had commiserated with Alistair's anxiety to keep the truth from Amelia.

'You and I know very well, sir, how cut up she'd be about it all. It's hard for a woman to understand these things — especially in relation to her only son. A mother wants to be proud, wouldn't you say? God knows, Duncan's done his best. No wonder he's hysterical at the idea of

184

your both knowing.'

'So,' Alistair said slowly, 'you've taken it upon yourself to shoulder the blame. Did my son ask you to do that?'

'Certainly not. He was in no condition to think straight about anything. The whole thing has reduced him to pulp. It was a good thing I had my wits about me. When we found the boy's note I knew what I had to do to save the situation.' Bernard paused. If he was waiting for thanks, none were forthcoming.

'It was hardly your responsibility.'

'It didn't seem that way to me, sir. At the time I thought my shoulders were broader than Duncan's, and I have no family to harm. Nobody would give a bugger — if you'll pardon the pun — for what happens to me. There's nobody I can disgrace. People's memories are short when one is obscure. If, on the other hand, one holds any kind of public office where one is in a position to juggle with people's destinies, a very small amount of pitch can stick and gum up the whole works. I know you wouldn't care a rap for public opinion alone, sir, but you have to think of Mrs Parry too. She has so many ambitions and hopes for both of you. I didn't reckon she could bear the double disappointment. Isn't the new chairmanship of Discol between you and David Lang's father? Do you imagine you'd get it if he knew Duncan had let his son die mutilated on that railway line?' Abandoning any pretence of politeness his voice was nakedly menacing.

Alistair's voice was cold. 'I shall and can repudiate your action.'

Bernard got up and walked casually about the room, peering at the prints on the wall, an antique ormolu clock on the mantelpiece, some guns in a case, as if he had never seen them before. 'You can if you wish to destroy Duncan, possibly your marriage. Mrs Parry will only tolerate a certain degree of failure.' He stared Alistair down relentlessly and the older man's eyes were the first to fall. Bernard had assessed them all faultlessly. Alistair, unwilling to put the structure of his family to a test he knew could be fatally damaging, hesitated, and forfeited his manhood.

There had, of course, been a price. The faded gaps on the wallpaper where those etchings had once hung testified to that, as had the gradual disappearance of treasures from other parts of the house over a long period of time. Their sale was accounted for to Amelia as a necessary hedge against inflation and the means of their maintaining

Falconers, on which Alistair had secretly taken out a second mortgage. In the same manner, he had taken specimens of their solid silver pieces of cutlery and had replicas made in plate, selling the originals two and three pieces at a time under Amelia's nose. Once started, it was impossible to go back, and with the passage of years his original motive for keeping Bernard quiet became more vital as Duncan's and his own career advanced. His moral punishment existed in Duncan's continued reverence of Bernard and Frances's reliance upon him when the débâcle had occurred. Alistair had been horrified when she had told him of the setting up of the Trust fund controlled by Bernard but dared not voice or give reasons for his disapproval. Knighted and revered, he had more to lose now than at the beginning of his thraldom, and somewhere along the line integrity had tarnished with expediency.

Yet he had been courageous once. Alistair got up from his desk and went to look in the glass-fronted medal case supported from a bracket on the wall behind him. Testifying to that fact, the Military Cross and bar, the Distinguished Service Cross and Oakleaves of mentions in dispatches from the Second World War lay embedded in black velvet, with later insignia won for commercial deeds. He tried to recall the acts of physical bravery for which they had been awarded, recollecting the honourable fear that had accompanied them and of which he had not been ashamed. The fear spawned of moral cowardice was corrupting and debilitating. He was too craven to release himself from Bernard's hold, yet he knew that, should the situation demand, he was still capable of the active courage that won medals.

Restlessly he paced between the furniture, waiting to ring Frances, postponing the event as long as he could. He had alienated her yesterday by his clumsy innuendoes about Bernard and he wished now he had either kept his mouth shut, or opened it years ago, which would have been much more to the point. When Frances had told him of Bernard's disinclination to sell the Midas shares, Alistair had begun to get the whiff of a rat strong enough to bring everything out into the open, and although he didn't know what good it could possibly do at this late stage, he had felt the responsibility to warn her. Through her hostility he had sensed the striking of a chord of doubt. He understood Frances well enough to know it would need to be resolved. There might be nothing sinister to discover, but in his present mood of premonitory despondency, Alistair feared the gathering forces of destruction. It was nearly nine o'clock and she would be expecting his call. He lifted the receiver to dial.

Frances answered quickly and he knew immediately by her voice that something was wrong. It held a high, breezy tone of false reassurance which was maintained over the generalizations but which faltered imperceptibly when he asked, 'What news about the money?'

'I shall need more time. It's difficult with Bernard away.'

'Have you spoken to him, or George Bruton?' It was a shot in the dark and when she hesitated he knew he had been right. 'Frances, have you explained our position to George?'

'As a matter of fact, I did see him today.'

'And?'

The question hung on the wire as Frances selected and rejected a number of lies. He had rung while she was still in a state of shock and improperly prepared.

'Frances. Is anything wrong?'

'I don't know. There may be. I don't know what to think.'

'Tell me.'

189

She swallowed. The strain of bearing it alone was suddenly too much. 'I went to Bernard's offices. George showed me our portfolio. Alistair, there's a handful of shares in it, nothing approaching what there ought to be and no sign of any other investments. George was adamant that there are no other relevant files. That was the lot. After what you said yesterday, it looks ugly. I couldn't put it out of my mind, but I still can't believe that what you suggested and what I'm trying not to suspect is true.' Her voice quavered, and she cleared her throat.

He said as gently as he could, 'I think you should be prepared for the worst, Frances.'

'Why?' It was a squeaky thread of sound.

'You asked me yesterday if I thought Bernard was a crook. I know he is.'

'No. If you knew that you wouldn't have let us become so entangled with him. You'd have spoken out before.'

'I was very wrong not to do so. There were reasons — all of them selfish.'

'What do you know?'

'It doesn't matter.'

'How could you?' The words came out singly on an immense effort.

'I'll never know. I can't forgive myself.' He felt immensely weary and angry and ashamed. 'What will you do?'

'I don't know. I suppose one should prosecute but that costs money, and if it's true, we haven't got any. I've had enough of courts and legal wrangles to last a lifetime, Alistair — and in any case, it's not just the money.' She broke down on a sob. 'I love him.'

Alistair, looking fatuously into the receiver at his end as if trying to fathom the materialized shape of her words, felt as if someone had cut off his legs at the knees. 'You can't,' was the first thing he could find to say.

'I can and do. I love him. I don't care what he's done.' She was crying softly.

'Is Bernard the man you told me about? The one you're leaving Duncan for?'

'Yes. I think I've always loved him.'

'You're wrong, Frances, you can't. You said he'd look after you. Look what he's done to you.'

'I don't care. I don't care. There'll be some explanation.'

'I don't doubt it,' he said grimly, but she paid no attention. He heard her blow her nose and her voice came across stronger.

'Alistair, promise me you'll do nothing until I've seen Bernard. I must give him a chance to clear himself. After that, God knows what will happen, but please say nothing to anyone until then.'

'Suppose he doesn't come back?'

As if she hadn't thought of that ever since this afternoon.

'I can't imagine living without him,' she said simply, the tears flowing again. 'I can't talk coherently now. I think I'd better ring off.'

'Frances, wait — ' He couldn't let her go like this, but she had cut him off.

★ ★ ★

His hands were trembling and his heart pumped as if he had been running fast. Over fifteen years' mounting rage against Bernard encapsulated in this one moment and he rose unsteadily, his attention captured by reflected light on the glass of the gun cabinet. Only half-conscious of his actions, he went across and opened it, running his hands down the greased barrels and smooth butts of two rook rifles which had been made into four-tens. He had picked them up at an old country house sale and had them converted, since when they had been coveted by Bernard who would have liked to have added them to his collection, except that they would have looked out of place among his pistols. He had settled instead for Alistair's revolver. Like everything else he fancied, he had come down and collected it one day. He had delighted in showing it to Alistair when the latter had delivered an instalment of cash to the flat in Brandon Court on one occasion. Bernard had had just about all there was to take, including Alistair's self-respect, his worldly goods, Duncan's money and now he'd got his oily hands on Frances. There had to be a limit. Alistair had told her he wasn't prepared to see her hurt any more. Taking out one of the rifles, he put it to his shoulder, peering down the sight and imagining the pleasure of blasting the smug expression off Bernard's face. He squeezed the trigger, then lowered the weapon thoughtfully. The germ of a better, more practical idea came to him. It would need planning but it was relatively simple, and with luck, without risk of detection. He replaced the gun and opened the drawer of a brass chest on top of the cabinet. In among a jumbled assortment of cartridges, string, weights and four-by-two lay a cardboard box containing four loose nine-millimetre Sten machine-gun bullets — like the medals, relics from a more glorious past. Alistair took them out and laid them on the top of the chest, along with a specially selected length of string to which he attached one of the ball-bearing-shaped weights and enough four-by-two to make a pull-through of the size he required. Shredding a piece of cotton gauze, he wound it experimentally around one of the bullets. It lay innocently in his palm where he closed his fingers over it, weighing it, as he mentally weighed his plan of action. His blood had cooled, his hand was steady, proving that his nerve for this sort of disciplined exercise had not atrophied. After he had prepared the equipment that he needed, he placed it in a small hessian bag with a drawstring top and slipped it into his jacket pocket. There followed a systematic check of all the drawers in the chest to make sure no other automatic ammunition remained. He sat down to make a mental appreciation of the situation.

# 13

Frances too was waiting and thinking. She had slept badly, if at all, on Friday night, and Saturday was a day full of petty irritations starting with Dolly.

'Frances — ' her voice came plaintively over the phone just after nine o'clock — 'you haven't forgotten you're coming to supper tonight?'

Frances, with a heart and head as heavy as lead and a mouth like the bottom of a parrot's cage after numerous nightcaps, none of which had been efficacious, assured her that she had indeed remembered.

'I don't quite know how I'm going to get to the fishmonger this morning. Saturdays are so crowded in the town and I shall have all the vegetables to carry.'

'Must you go in? We don't have to have fish. Can't we have something simple. Bacon and eggs will do.'

'I think I can do a little better than that. I know I don't give grand dinner-parties like you are used to, Frances, but I do know how to lay a nice table and cook a decent meal.' Dolly's voice was prim and reproving with an accusation of condescension.

Frances bit her tongue. 'What I meant was, don't make a production of it. Haven't you got anything in the freezer?'

'I suppose I have, but not what I planned. Fish needs to be freshly bought. It's at times like this when I envy you your car. Still, I wouldn't ask you to put yourself out for me.'

'I'm sorry, Dolly, I can't anyway. I have to go in to the shop and that's in the opposite direction. There's a tangle that must be sorted out.'

The familiar self-pitying whine grated on Frances's over-stretched nerves.

'Of course. You're too busy for your old maid sister. Forget I asked. I'm lucky you're free tonight.'

'I look forward to it,' said Frances with as much cheerfulness as she could muster. 'Eight o'clock. All news then.' She put the phone down with relief and went in search of the aspirin bottle.

★ ★ ★

The problem at the shop involved a lost parcel of bedspreads for a special order which had been dispatched by train and had either to be traced or replaced by the following Wednesday. By the time Frances had placated the customer, put a rocket behind British Rail who had siphoned off her enquiries through umpteen departments, and laid on an overtime workforce to make the re-order, her temper was short and her stamina low.

'You look rough,' Liz commented, coming through the office at the end of the morning.

Frances felt it. Rough and no readier to face what lay before her at six o'clock than she had been yesterday. She had rehearsed a variety of opening lines, not daring to believe that Bernard would be there to hear them. During the afternoon she resisted the temptation of phoning his flat to see if he had returned early. At half past four she had a bath and changed and washed her hair, adorning herself in Bernard's favourite blue like a sacrificial lamb.

★ ★ ★

The evening was prematurely overcast with grey clouds deepening the twilight. By the time Frances left No. 6 it was raining, and as she turned off the emptying shopping streets into the seclusion of Brandon Court she was reminded of that first time she and Bernard had come here together. The

197

weather had been equally sombre and the offices had worn their shuttered weekend faces as they did now. There was no other car in the street. If Bernard were home he could have garaged the Citroën in the mews behind the house. If he were home. Frances drove round there now and parked the Mini at the end of the cutting, as was her custom, where it was concealed from passers-by. She doused the lights of the car, then locked it, sheltered by a heavily spattered umbrella. Bernard's key admitted her to the lobby and when she pressed the button for the lift, its doors opened immediately. If he were back, surely it would not be at ground level. He would have taken it up to the third floor and left it there, unless he had thought of her coming and returned it for her convenience. Ascending, Frances steeled herself for the confirmation of all her doubts by his absence. The lift whined to a halt and two seconds later she was across the hall and had inserted the key of his front door into its lock.

The first things to hit her were Bernard's coat slung over the banister and his briefcase in the stairwell. The kitchen and drawing-room doors were open and the sound of a radio came from away upstairs. The overwhelming relief of these signs of his presence was intoxicating enough to render Frances's legs like jelly, and she leaned with her back against the closed door, her eyes shut in a weak prayer of gratitude that he hadn't deserted her. The events of the preceding days were an impossible nightmare. Her imagination had run riot, and as for Alistair's — it just went to show how dangerously one could be influenced, when emotionally vulnerable, by half-baked prejudice and innuendo. She shook her umbrella and, dropping it into a brass shell case which stood there for the purpose, crossed the hall and put her foot on the bottom stair. Bernard must have heard her because the radio was turned down and his voice called from above, 'Frances, is that you?'

'Yes.'

'Come up.'

She entered the bedroom as he was coming out of the bathroom, freshly bathed, his hair still wet, wearing a knee-length towelling coat which he was in the act of securing with a tie-belt.

'I was tired and filthy. Better now.' He came to her and put his arms around her waist. 'Much better now.' He kissed her openly and deeply and her treacherous senses responded as hungrily as if she had been starved of him for five years rather than days. Eventually he pulled back from her, gratified and amused. 'You've obviously missed me as much as I have you.'

'Have you missed me?'

'Can't you tell?' He drew her against him to emphasize the proof of his statement and they kissed again with increasing passion as he manoeuvred her back towards the bed. The brass rail cutting across her shoulders brought her back to sanity, and with an effort she disengaged herself from his embrace.

'Not so fast.'

'Why not? It's what you're here for, isn't it, and we've only got — what — an hour and a quarter. A quarter less than you promised me.'

'I've got to talk to you first.' She moved away from him across to the dressing-table where she rearranged his ivory-backed brushes, not knowing how to start.

'Fire away then.' He sat down on the bed, then swung his legs up and lay back, his arms clasped behind his head. The position was relaxed, even jaunty, with no trace of the wariness that flickered briefly behind his eyes at her tone.

She turned to face him. 'Before you went away you said you'd tell George to get on with the sale of those Midas shares. Why didn't you do as I asked?'

The moment had come and there was no point in hedging. Bernard licked his lips. 'I imagine you've been in touch with him.'

She nodded. 'Yesterday. He showed me our portfolio.'

'You know why then.' He could see that his easy admission had astounded her. 'What's the point of lying, Fran? I shan't insult you by doing that.'

'You've managed to do so all the time Duncan's been in gaol,' she exclaimed. 'Do you expect me to accept calmly the fact that you've swindled him out of over £100,000? That is what you're saying?'

'I didn't know how you'd take it.'

'Or care, I presume,' she said tartly, stung by his apparent disinterest in her reaction.

He sighed, and abandoned his nonchalant position, getting off the bed and going to find a packet of cigarettes and a lighter in the pockets of the suit he had recently discarded. 'It's true, I didn't care to start with. I just wanted the money. But I do now. Feeling as I do about you now, I couldn't do you out of anything. I never thought of the money as yours at the time. I didn't know I was going to fall in love with you. But it can be yours now that you're staying with me and not going back to him.'

Frances sat down weakly on the dressing-table stool. Catapulted into this Alice in Wonderland reasoning, she wondered whether it was she or Bernard who qualified for certification.

'You mean that you want me to become an accessory after the fact and we both make off with the money stolen from Duncan?'

'Put crudely, that is the picture.' He leaned against the brass bed support and she could see that he was completely serious.

'And what about him?'

'What about him?' He spat the words with venom and their animosity surprised Frances as much as had Alistair's when he had revealed his true feelings towards Bernard. Recognizably stable relationships had become suddenly topsy-turvy with menacing portent. 'You remember the story of the talents in the Bible, Fran? Duncan buried his. I used mine. He deserves nothing. Where is he today in spite of all his advantages? He couldn't have made more of a balls of his life if he'd been in my position with none of them. What had I got? No home, no money, parents who invested in their own salvation serving a mythical ideal rather than in their son's future. How do you imagine I felt when I saw everything made smooth for him, all the chances he had from which I could have benefited twice, three times as much? There are winners and losers, Fran. I told you before, one takes what one wants. Nobody's yet handed me anything on a platter.'

She looked at him as if she had never seen him before. 'You're sick,' she said wonderingly. 'You won at his expense. It satisfied your personal vendetta of jealousy and envy, didn't it? And I was part of it. You only wanted me because I was his.'

He shook his head. 'That's how it began. I admit it. But not now. We've got something very special, Fran. Together we can both be rid of Duncan. You love me.'

'You're crazy. You can't seriously have thought I'd steal.'

'It isn't stealing. The money's yours.'

'It's not mine and it's certainly not yours by right.'

'The spoils of war.'

'That's lunatic reasoning. Duncan didn't even know he was fighting.'

'He doesn't know the meaning of the word. All his life somebody else has fought for him.'

'It doesn't make it acceptable. It's criminal. You'll go to prison yourself. So would I.'

'I think not.'

'Of course you will.'

Bernard reached over and stubbed his

cigarette out in an ashtray on the dressing-table before answering. 'If the fear of arrest is all that's stopping you, forget it. Neither Duncan, nor Sir Alistair — ' he said it mockingly, the emphasis upon the title — 'will be anxious to prosecute in this case.' He had regained his suavity and Frances felt a chilling warning stab of fear. Of course there had to be a missing piece of the whole incomprehensible puzzle for it to make sense. With morbid certainty she knew the picture was going to be even uglier. Against all her inclinations she asked, 'Why?'

'The old boy's been paying me hush money for years. Ever since Cambridge in fact.'

She sat gaping at him with all the appearance of stupidity.

'I did him a favour covering up for Duncan. I saved his son's skin and his own. If the truth had been known would he have got that chairmanship in preference to David Lang's father? I doubt it. Would he have got his knighthood? Unlikely, wouldn't you say? It would break her ladyship's heart to have that little lot come out.'

'Blackmail?'

'A business arrangement. I had a commodity to sell. I can see I've shocked you. I told you there were warts.'

Staring at him, she said, 'You haven't any morals, have you?'

He shrugged without shame. 'My father lived a moral life. It didn't do a lot for my mother or for me. Everyone makes a moral of expediency. It was expedient for me to do what I could for myself. You're half-way there too. You've convinced yourself you're justified in leaving Duncan. And so you are. You still want to come to me. I can see it in your eyes. You'll find a reason why you should. Perhaps your mission is to save me from myself.' He smiled cynically. 'The only difference between us is that I am honest.'

She hotly repudiated the grain of uncomfortable truth. 'You're twisted. You're the cripple. It's you that needs the crutches. You didn't need our money. It was your way of getting back at life. I could have understood that — loved you in spite of it. But what you've done to Alistair, that's unforgivable. How you must have hated them under all the pretence of friendship.'

'He did it to himself through vanity and cowardice. Snobbery, arrogance, laziness and weakness aren't attractive attributes either, only they aren't against the law. Maybe they should be. They're anti-social and do enough damage.'

'What about their kindness and trust which you abused?'

'I saved them their reputations in return. Fran, we're splitting hairs. Don't pretend you didn't know what sort of a person I am. I can't be accused of not saying what I think.'

'I didn't believe you meant half of it,' she said helplessly. 'I'm muddled and confused. How could I have believed you loved me?' She stood up in her agitation.

'Because I do.'

'But you're a liar — a thief.'

'You are also a liar and an adulteress. But I don't assume you have no virtues. Nobody's all good.' He smiled again, this time insidiously, with tender candour. He was too damned plausible with his warped morality and the wicked way he made her heart turn over and her body weak for him, despite what she had learned. Thinking of Alistair, she felt sick — of Duncan, sad — of the money, angry — but of herself, disgusted that her desire for Bernard hadn't automatically been killed stone dead. He was evil, most likely psychotic. It was the kindest explanation for the sustained premeditated campaign that he had waged. He had cleverly turned all their weaknesses to his account, arrogantly confident that he ran no serious risk of denouncement.

He watched her irresolution. 'What are you going to do?'

'I don't know.' Nor did she.

'Why should it make any difference to us? I love you, Fran. I've never had anyone of my own before. We only live once.'

'Don't.'

'If you want proof, I'll give all the money back. Duncan can have his future and your conscience will be easy.'

The strange expression in her eyes could have been pity as they filled with tears.

'Fran. Darling.' He pulled her into his arms and started kissing her. 'It won't seem so bad in the morning. Don't leave me.'

'Please let me go.' She struggled free before the tears or his persuasions won. 'I must leave.' She remembered her supper date and looked at her watch. The hands stood at seven. She must get out of here and somewhere — anywhere to collect her thoughts and her composure before facing *Sole bonne femme* with Dolly. Strange how at every crisis in her life the mundane intruded. She remembered how at her mother's funeral the thought uppermost in her mind was where to find the best teaspoons for the tea-party to follow.

Bernard released her. Better let her go.

She'd be back. Another couple of minutes just now and she would have capitulated, but better to play it cannily.

'Don't come down.' The absurdity of tidying off such a scene with social politenesses brought her to the verge of hysteria. In the handy way of playwrights it should have been terminated by fade-out on a dramatic line, but in real life people had to live between situations as best they could. In spite of her protestation he went with her to the door and saw her out. Closing it when she had gone, he stood waiting, half expecting a second thought to bring her back, but nothing happened and he shrugged his shoulders. There was nothing she could do immediately. She'd never go to the police. He was sure enough of that.

A cold draught blew across the hall and around his bare legs and Bernard shivered. The warmth of his bath had worn off and with the drama of the past hour he had forgotten his lightly clad condition. It was more of a breeze than a draught. The drawing-room door threatened to slam and he stepped across its threshold, illuminated in the darkened room by a shaft of light from the hall. He must have left a window open somewhere. The french doors at the far end of the room rattled. He raised his hand to the light switch, but before he could reach it the blast of a bullet caught him high up in the chest. There was no pain, just the fleeting force of the impact which spun him round and felled him face downwards on the carpet, his features set in a macabre death mask of astonishment.

★ ★ ★

There was a mirror in the lift in which Frances surveyed her reflection. Except for a lack of lipstick, she didn't look any different. There was no outward sign of the turmoil in her heart and brain. She repainted her mouth and touched the lashes under her eyes which had smudged with tears. The night outside was black, the rain coming down cats and dogs, and she realized she had no protection against it. She'd left her umbrella in Bernard's shell case upstairs. Frances hesitated. She didn't want to go back, neither did she relish getting soaked nor losing the umbrella which had been a recent present from Liz. It was just inside the flat. If she nipped up and opened the door she could slip it out without Bernard knowing she had returned. Stepping back into the lift, she pressed the third-floor button once more, alighting at the apartment.

The key turned silently and she stealthily tiptoed forward, an eye and one ear cocked towards the stairs. A sound to her right caused her to whirl guiltily round and she froze in uncomprehending, horrified shock at the sight before her.

Alistair stood a foot inside the drawing-room with a revolver in his gloved hand. Inconsequentially, she recognized the gloves as those he wore for driving. She had noticed them that day in the car and reflected that not many modern men wore them. He had on a dark raincoat over dark trousers. If she clung to similar futilities of thought she might escape grappling for the reason that Bernard was lying so still on the carpet behind him. Something about his attitude told her that he wasn't going to get up. She put her hand over her mouth like a ham actress registering surprise, but in her case it was to prevent herself being sick.

# 14

Alistair was the first to speak. 'Get out and away from here, Frances,' he said.

She pushed past him to get to Bernard and went down on her knees beside the body. There was a hole in the back of his bath robe near his left shoulder-blade, but otherwise no mess around it. The blood was coming from a wound invisible to her, its dark stain mingling with the pattern on the carpet, and she put out a hand to turn him over to see the extent of the damage.

'Don't touch him. Don't touch anything,' Alistair curtly ordered.

'He may not be dead.'

'He's dead.' The flat finality of his voice brought the reality home like a sharp slap.

'Oh my God! Oh Christ! Bernard!' She started shaking as with an uncontrollable ague and stumbled as she tried to rise to her feet, but her legs wouldn't support her. 'Oh dear God!'

'Here. Lean on me.' He gave her his arm and led her to a chair. He still had the gun in his hand and she shrank from it as he assisted her. 'It's all right. It won't go off again.'

At his choice of words a fragile hope awakened in her breast that she had mis-read the tableau she had surprised on entering. 'Is that what happened? It went off?' Her teeth were chattering and her lips felt peculiarly numb. It was a tremendous effort forming the syllables.

Ignoring her question, he said, 'You'd better have a drink.' He went to a table just beyond the perimeter of light in which they could see one another and fetched a bottle of whisky which he uncapped and held to her mouth. 'No time for frills or washing up.'

She swallowed with difficulty, her tongue getting in the way of the narrow opening, but a draught of the liquid went down, burning her throat, warming her stomach and steadying her nerves. In spite of the dark, Alistair seemed to know his way around. He wiped the neck of the bottle and replaced it, then came and stood over her.

'Did it go off?' she asked again.

'Not by mistake. I shot him.' His tone was matter of fact, even businesslike.

'Not deliberately.'

'Quite deliberately. I should have done it years ago.'

'You planned this?'

'I worked it out — what I thought might

212

be a feasible scheme. After you told me that he was your lover I knew I had to do something.'

'But — murder?' It was improbable associating the act with the tolerant, gentle, kindly Alistair of her acquaintance. She had lately thought of him as fragile and declining but the man standing beside her exuding purpose and authority was acting with the calm dispatch of a stranger. Her whole world was suddenly peopled with strangers.

'He deserved it. He was scum. I murdered men in the war with this, innocent men. They gave me medals for it.' As he spoke he broke open the gun and removed the cartridge case of the spent bullet from its chamber. This he slipped into his pocket, then rested the weapon on the arm of her chair. From the other pocket he produced the pull-through he had prepared, and another cloth. Frances recognized the revolver Bernard had shown her.

'That's the gun you gave him,' she said stupidly, the situation still unreal.

'The one he took,' Alistair said grimly.

'They'll trace it to you.'

'Not a chance. It's been hanging here too long. I never had a firearms certificate for it. Bernard may or may not have included it on his along with the other pistols. In any

213

case, no one is going to suspect that this was the weapon used. It's going back on the wall — all clean and tidy.' He punctuated the words by tugging the four-by-two through the barrel twice, three times, then wiping the revolver carefully all over with the duster. Stepping casually over Bernard's corpse, he inspected the barrel minutely against the light in the hall, then, apparently satisfied, clicked it back into position. 'Clean as a whistle.'

'They'll know from the bullet.'

'I think not. You see, Frances, this is a .38 calibre rimfire revolver. The bullet they will find will be an automatic weapon bullet, nine-millimetre Sten gun to be precise, rimless. The gun they'll be looking for will therefore be an automatic, one the intruder brought with him and took away again. Even in the improbable likelihood they trace this gun to me, I possess no ammunition to fit it, nor any of the type they will discover has killed Bernard. Two rook rifles are the only weapons I own. Do I make myself clear?'

'How can you fire the wrong bullet?'

'By the simple expedient of wrapping some fibres of gauze around it. A piece of grass or corn would have done as well.' He withdrew the cartridge and held it out for her inspection under torchlight. Some singed cotton threads adhered to the metal.

214

'They'll think of that. If you did, they will.'

'They may, but they can't prove it. Ideally, the cartridge case should be left for them to find. It would have been ejected just about here if the bullet had come from an automatic.' Alistair went and stood over a little to the right of the body, looking down as if reconsidering his best course of action. 'On the other hand, I think not.' He pocketed the case again. 'These ballistics boys can tell too much from the slightest scratch. With no cartridge case they may be suspicious but there's still no proof.'

Frances's brain, sharpening with every second, stirred to the immediate danger of his predicament. 'You mustn't stay here.'

'No.' He looked at his watch. 'It's seven-fifteen. I must be back at the club by seven twenty-eight. I'm lecturing at the Trafalgar rooms tonight — youth recruitment into industry. At seven-thirty prompt Amelia will hammer on the door behind which I'm closeted with the tape-recorder going over my speech. She promised me half an hour's peace while she bathed and had her hair brushed out.' He opened his coat and Frances saw in the dim light that underneath it he wore dress trousers and an evening shirt. His audacity staggered her.

215

'Isn't it a rather hackneyed alibi? I imagine the police read Agatha Christie.'

'Best I could do on the spur of twenty-four hours. Nobody saw me leave the club. Fortuitously placed, only a stone's throw from here. I knew I could nip up the fire-escape and lay my hands on the gun immediately. You told me Bernard would be back at six. Surprise achieved the rest. I was going to make it look like a break-in. Your appearance has complicated matters.'

He regarded her worriedly. The realization of her involvement suddenly came home to him, having the same effect as the snapping of a hypnotist's fingers to bring his patient out of a trance. The euphoria that had sustained him through the act fell away and urgency and fright were taking its place. To quell her own panic, Frances took charge.

'We still can.' The adrenalin was flowing once more as the consciousness of their shared peril and necessity for haste superseded the horror of the situation. 'Put the gun back. Can you see?'

With the aid of the flashlight Alistair crossed the room to replace the revolver on its hook. The beam glinted on slivers of broken glass lying inside the french window on the carpet under a hole in the pane where he had put his fist through to unlock the frame and secure his entry.

'Give me the duster.' He handed it over and, using it to protect the furniture from her fingerprints, Frances started randomly opening drawers in the desk and tables, spilling their contents all over the floor. He came up behind her, shining the light, taking care not to let it be seen from beyond the undrawn curtains. The glass and steel sculpture, standing alone, caught her eye and invited vandalism. Smashing it would afford her a vindictive pleasure and lend credulity to the idea of a burglary. In the act of reaching for it, an instantaneous memory stayed her hand. The thing lying on the floor was incapable of speech, but clearly Frances heard Bernard's voice:

'I've already been caught once with it setting off the alarm. It was on the window-seat — twenty-five minutes to reach the point when all the arms are extended.'

The alarm. That was it. It would give them twenty minutes' grace and by that time she and Alistair could be at their appointed rendezvous, he mingling with the pre-prandial cocktail crowd who had come to hear his lecture, she in Dolly's flat in Richmond.

'I can give us both a better alibi. I know how to set the burglar alarm so that it will go off after we've left here.'

'How?'

'It doesn't matter how. Leave it to me. You must go quickly. All you have to do is to be sure to be among people from the moment you return to the club. The alarm will go off near enough at five to eight. The police will be here by the hour. It will have been set off by a burglar putting his hand through the window. Hurry, now — go.'

'I can't leave you here with all this.'

She resisted looking in the direction of Bernard's body. 'You must. Hurry. Trust me. I'm all right. I know exactly what to do.'

'Supposing you're seen? Supposing it doesn't work? I shan't know what's happened to you.'

She thought swiftly. 'Make an excuse to drop in to No. 6 on your way home tomorrow. That will be natural enough. Don't ring, though.' She was firmly in command and it was he who now dithered and needed bracing.

'Frances, I can't.'

'For Christ's sake stop arguing and go. You've got five minutes before Amelia will be at that door.'

'Shall I leave the torch?'

'No. Just keep your head.' She watched the

beam travel before him, then extinguish itself as he reached the french window. 'Don't step on the glass,' she called softly. She heard the click of the latch as he slipped out on to the fire-escape, then he was gone.

* * *

Alone, cold panic threatened to spiral, but Frances fought it down and marshalled her thoughts into sequence. There were details, like the glass, to concentrate upon in the next six minutes. The french window must remain unlocked, this room and the bedroom wiped clean as possible of her earlier prints. With the duster she did a cursory polish of any wooden chair arms, glass or other surfaces she might have touched. To circumvent Bernard required a Promethean effort of will, but her instinct for survival negated the primitive fear of passing the inert bundle by the door. Gathering her skirts against her legs as though fearful that any moment he might extend a hand and grab her ankle, she edged warily into the hall and ran upstairs, wiping the banisters en route. The bedroom was as he and she had left it. Beads of water from his recent bath had not yet dried upon the porcelain, the radio still playing under its breath, the curtains drawn. Frances ran the cloth over the bedstead, side tables, dressing-table and stool, then turned down the counterpane, her imagination assisting her in the setting of the scene. Bernard returned from a few days from home, had decided on a relaxing bath and an early night, perhaps reading or working on some papers in bed. He had retired to his bedroom and was preparing to settle down to a peaceful evening, after setting the downstairs alarm circuit, when someone entering the drawing-room by the fire-escape had set it off. Running downstairs to try to catch the culprit, he had been shot on entering the room. Frances frowned. Papers. Briefcase. She had seen it at the base of the stairs. She went swiftly down and fetched it, carrying it carefully, its handle wrapped in the duster, and put it by the bed. Leaving the light on and the door open, she descended once more.

In the kitchen, which she dusted for luck, she found hanging from a clothes peg a pair of rubber gloves. It would be handier to wear them for the last part of the action. She carefully closed the kitchen door. She was breathless, her heart beating in the stepped-up rhythm required to run through her tasks at speed. Once more she had to pass the corpse and this time, conscious of

220

time running out, she stepped over it as Alistair had done. She went over to the sculpture, lifted it from the table Bernard had eventually bought for it, arranged it on the window-seat, testing the extended length of the longest arm by lifting it gently with one finger. It tipped the window-pane. Gently she pressed the arms downwards as low as they would go. All ready. Her watch said 7.30 exactly. Frances straightened, then paused, debating upon the best place to switch it on. The weakest part of her plan was that she couldn't be sure how long the sculpture would be in action until somebody turned it off. During that time it might fully extend several times, touching the window and arousing suspicion that the alarm had been triggered from there and not the french window, but she could only trust to luck that all the attentions of the police would be focused on the broken window. She reflected ironically that if Alistair had given her ten years instead of a bare ten minutes to dream up an alibi she might have done better. A certain amount would have to be left to chance.

Both switches by the door being in the up position, she decided that setting the sculpture going by its own switch might call less attention to its having been deliberately turned on. Holding her breath for the countdown, she pressed the button, crossed the room taking Bernard in her stride, went out into the hall closing the door behind her, and made for the cupboard under the stairs. The knob switching off the upstairs circuit clicked easily to the left. The warning buzzer obediently responded to the turn of her key. Frances emerged from the cupboard and shut the door. She mustn't leave anything behind this time. Umbrella. Handbag. Duster. She had them all. She slipped out of the flat and locked the door, ran to the lift and was about to descend when she remembered her own thoughts about its positioning on coming to meet Bernard this evening. To give her alibi extra authenticity the lift must remain on the third floor. Stairs! Fighting down a sob of pure panic, she stepped out of the elevator, leaving its doors ajar, and ran to the end of the hall where an asbestos door provided the only other means of egress. She'd never used the staircase before, but common sense dictated that one must exist. Sure enough, the door gave on to a flight which broadened with every floor descended until it ended in an extravagant sweep on the marbled hallway to the main offices. To the left there was another fire door whose position suggested that it should give on to Bernard's private lobby. Sweating and praying that it wouldn't be locked, Frances pushed, and found herself in that familiar territory. The minimal hitch coupled with the run downstairs had unnerved her, but time was her enemy and she couldn't afford the luxury of a moment's rest.

She didn't remove the rubber gloves until she was behind the wheel of the Mini. Somewhere along the line her keys to Bernard's flat must be disposed of. There was no car or bystander to see her emerge from the mews, and only one taxi disappearing round the opposite side of the rectangle as she came into Belgrave Square. Resisting an impulse to put her foot down and drive like the clappers away from the nightmare that lay behind, she resolutely adhered to the speed limit until she came to an unrestricted zone of dual carriageway where the city retreated into suburbia and every moment took her closer to safety. Never would she be so thankful to see Dolly. She kept looking at her watch as she timed the journey, and all along the route hitherto unnoticed clock faces on factories, churches and shops thrust their illuminated commentaries into her consciousness.

Frances had been travelling for exactly twenty-two minutes by the time she swung into the forecourt of the flats in Amberton

Close. Drawing to a halt, she slumped wearily in her seat with relief and in preparation for the continuing ordeal. Never look back. Don't look back. Don't remember. Don't regret. Above all, don't cry or be sick. She got out of the car and rang Dolly's bell. Any minute now another bell would be ringing, followed doubtless by police sirens and the blue flashing lights of the ambulance. They'd cover Bernard with a blanket and carry him away on a stretcher. Don't look forward either. Try not to think at all.

The door swung open. 'You're early for once, Frances. How nice that you had nothing better to do.'

★ ★ ★

In the control room of police headquarters 'A' Division, a red light flashed on the alarm board and its appearance at 7.56 p.m. was recorded by PC John Donovan. Using the pencil in his right hand, with his left he reached for the intercom, while his eyes scanned a London road map above him which charted the courses and territories of a fleet of Panda cars.

'Control room to Panda four-five-zero-eight. Control room to Panda four-five-zero-eight — over.'

The response was immediate. 'Four-five-zero-eight — over.'

'Direct burglar alarm warning, 76 Brandon Court, off Belgrave Square. Better get along there and see if it's a break-in or a false alarm.'

'We're on our way.'

In the Panda car PC Dick Brinker switched off his receiver and nodded affirmatively at the driver who was cruising down Earls Court Road. The rain had cleared most people off the streets and their progress was unimpeded as they crossed over into Redcliffe Gardens, then turned left into the Fulham Road. A blast of the siren was necessary approaching the intersection at Brompton Road and Pont Street, then they were into the square and round the one-way system, drawing up in front of 76 Brandon Court at 8.01 precisely. Jack Parsons remained in the driving seat, while Brinker jumped out and with the aid of a torch scanned the name plates on the front door of the building. He came back and thrust his head through the car window. It was necessary to shout above the penetrating cacophony of the alarm siren.

'It's the flat upstairs. You cover this entrance. I'll go round and see if there's any evidence of a break-in.'

'OK.' Parsons's reaction was laconic. Nine times out of ten it was a false alarm — a fault in the system or a door carelessly closed. It would be hard luck on any neighbours if the silly buggers had gone away for the weekend and this banshee had to be endured until they returned on Monday. He too got out of the car, turning up his collar against the elements, and stood on the pavement facing the house.

Brinker had disappeared into an alleyway to the right. He played his torch over some downstairs windows obviously belonging to offices, which appeared intact and firmly secured. There was a fire-escape, and then beyond the side of the house the alley finished in a dead end, both sides highly walled. Retracing his steps, he climbed a few rungs of the metal ladder from which vantage point he shone the light into the garden on the other side of the wall, but there was no evidence of anything untoward. The higher he went, the more intensified became the ear-splitting wail of the siren. The first-and second-floor windows reflected the torch beam back at him sightlessly and his breath was uneven as he made the landing-stage at the third and came across the gash in the glass of the french window. Standing back, half protected by the wall,

Brinker called out, 'This is the police. We're coming in.' He felt pretty foolish doing so as he could hardly hear his own voice in the deafening presence of the alarm. He doubted whether any burglar would have hung around in the face of that racket. He would have had to be slippy, but six minutes was all the average villain required and he could have nipped out the way he had come, down the escape and over the end wall, just missing their own arrival. Gingerly, Brinker directed the torch beam through the hole in the window-pane, and when there was no immediate reaction from within, he took courage and played it right into the room. The state of disorder that met his eye was an all too familiar one. Unbuttoning the flap of his breast pocket, he spoke into his transmitter.

'It's a break-in all right, Jack. Up on the third floor. I'm just going in.'

The french window gave to pressure on the handle and Brinker stepped inside, over as much of the glass as he could see on the carpet but unavoidably feeling the crunch of particles under his boots. He advanced cautiously, then as no attacker materialized, more boldly, instinctively heading for the door where he could shed more light upon the scene and discover as soon as possible how to stop that bloody siren. There was a peculiar light half-way up the room near the window, which on a cursory inspection looked like some weird kind of carousel — one of those fashionable executive toys that people gave men who already had everything. It had branches which dipped in a sinking *rallentando* movement.

Brinker's foot hit the edge of an upturned desk drawer and he stumbled clumsily over it, propelled forward, his hand directing the circle of light jerkily across the carpet. Unexpectedly Bernard's body loomed into spot at the same moment as Parsons's breathless voice reached him in a shout above the continuing din.

'Are you all right, Dick?'

Brinker completed his journey. The back edge of his hand contacted the two switches by the door and pressed them both down. 'I am, but it doesn't look as if this poor bleeder is.' Brinker opened the door into the hall and went swiftly through the rest of the apartment. It was obvious that the intruder had confined his activities to the one room and had been caught red-handed. Once assured that he wasn't lurking anywhere on the premises, Brinker applied his penknife to the screws holding the casing of the alarm control panel, then a wire and a degree of brute force to the apparatus revealed. The siren cut off.

'Thank God for that.' He got up off his knees from inside the hall cupboard and emerged, dusting off his trousers. 'You stay here. I'll go and radio for the Path and fingerprint boys. It looks like no nookie tonight for any of us.'

Left alone, Parsons took stock of the room and its contents. Whoever he was, the victim had been a man of taste, a connoisseur of antiques — and of firearms. The policeman cast an appreciative eye over the display of pistols. No shortage of a possible weapon, assuming one could lay one's hands on the appropriate ammunition, which would be unlikely in the case of the earlier models. They would need more time to load than their villain had had at his disposal. The Smith and Wesson could be a possibility, but almost too obvious a one. In six minutes a burglar would have been pushed to have made his entry, turned the room over and had the presence of mind to take down and use the revolver, retaining the necessary element of surprise. And if it wasn't a burglar but a premeditated crime by someone who had known of the presence of the gun and made the job look like a house-breaking, the same time factor applied. He moved away to study a Chinese vase and bowl which his fingers itched to touch. Jack Parsons's hobby was china and glass, ancient and modern. Take that funny-looking ornament with its dangling bits and bobs. Some people might detest it for its peculiarly unsymmetrical modernity, but for him the combination of rough cut glass with steel was beautiful. It had a switch on it and was probably meant to light up. He'd seen anemone-type ornaments in shop displays, their porcupine steel spines lit and changing colour — the same kind of principle. He was brought back to earth by Brinker's reappearance.

Half an hour later Bernard's body had been removed to the mortuary, having been photographed from every angle and its position chalk-marked on £20,000 worth of carpet. The police photographer had brought arc lights for the purpose which he had placed in position, casting his eye around for suitable power points in which to plug them. One he found near the fireplace, another in the skirting by the window-seat. Removing the sculpture plug and that of an electric clock from their sockets, he inserted those of the arc lights and took his pictures. When he had finished he unplugged his lamps and departed in haste, anxious only to get the photographs developed quickly enough for him to return to the arms from whence he had reluctantly been prised in off-duty time. The owner's husband would be home after early night shift, so there was no point in wasting precious moments.

# 15

An interminable night was being succeeded by a comparably endless day, to which Frances had awoken after a single exhausted hour's sleep. God alone knew how she had endured the meal with Dolly, and afterwards sat watching television. The humdrum formula of a thousand other such visits rendered the events of the earlier part of the evening even more totally incredible. She was an accessory to murder, and yet here she was discussing the price of bloaters and applauding a snub Dolly had administered to a trainee in counter service as though these were considerations of consequence. Frances concentrated on the mental effort of appearing an attentive participant as if her life depended upon it — as it very well might! She must betray no preoccupation nor depression of spirits which might afterwards be remembered, the source of which to be questioned. Questions there would undoubtedly be, and come to that, she had a few insoluble ones of her own.

Alone at last, back at No. 6, they came crowding in to plague her as, sleep impossible, she sat up through the night. Bernard was dead. The enormity of that one fact seemed to have bludgeoned her faculty for emotion into paralysis. Some time when the numbness wore off, there would be a secret gehenna to be endured, but for the moment it was the urgency of Alistair's position that primarily entertained her. It was inconceivable to think of him as a murderer. Kind, gentle Alistair, dominated by Amelia, paying up all those years rather than upset her. His enemies would say he had been motivated by his own ambition, but Frances knew this to have been a lesser impetus. He had taken the law into his own hands, as Duncan had done in the case of Ellen, and she was angry with him for it, as she had been angry with Duncan. She was in an impossible position. True, he hadn't intended to involve her, but now not only was she involved but she bore responsibility for his safety as well as her own. Unreasonably she felt she should have been given more time to work out a foolproof plan. He had been coolly confident enough about the police not connecting the gun with the bullet, and she could only pray that his sanguinity would prove justified. She felt a great deal less assured about their hastily contrived alibi. There were a number of intangibles, not the least being if and when the sculpture had been switched off, or on again, and if the latter, might it not repeat its performance in triggering off the alarm should the police reset the siren? Her knowledge of criminal procedure was sketchy, but was it not their practice to leave the scene of a murder guarded and cordoned off? The alarm would surely not be reset in these circumstances. What were the two things they always looked for — opportunity and motive? With a slice of luck she and Alistair might get away with the lack of the former — but motive was another ball game.

Frances lit another cigarette from the dying butt in her mouth, then transferred the end to the ashtray by her elbow which was already more than half full. She shut her eyes and concentrated on enumerating their joint motives. There was the blackmail — but nobody knew about that except themselves. They were safe enough on that count. Equally unpublicized was her liaison with Bernard. No reason why that should come out. The biggest and insuperable stumbling block was the money. Whichever way one looked at it, the fact of its absence could not be concealed from Duncan. He was coming out of prison in less than three weeks, expecting to launch a business with his greatly enhanced capital which no longer existed. Her mind sidetracked into ramified complications. They would be entirely dependent upon the shop. He couldn't refuse now to come into partnership with her and Liz, and having Hobson's choice foisted upon him needs must create perilous pressures. Bernard had been Duncan's hero. Telling him that he was dead was going to be bad enough, but shattering the illusion of his friend's honour would be ten times worse, and anyway, such a course left her at square one, with a possible motive for murder should the police go that far. If she told Duncan that Bernard was a shit and had swindled them out of everything, she could logically be supposed to be enraged enough to want to see him dead. And she had visited the offices of Bruton and King only the previous day, an occurrence unusual enough in itself to create suspicion. George would be sure to tell them, innocently enough, but it could look bad. Frances toyed with the practicability of confessing to Duncan that she had withdrawn the money herself for her own business, or mismanaged it in some way, but rejected that as too flimsy and out of character as Duncan knew her.

Her brain tangled with the implications of the moves open to her and finding them all unsatisfactory, she cleared it and attempted a fresh avenue. If you were going to lie — and she was already steeped in blood too far — keeping as near to the truth as possible lent falsehood a spurious verisimilitude. Bernard had had the money. Supposing she were to say he had received it as a loan, with her approval. Soon after Duncan had been confined, Bernard had confided to Frances that he was in some kind of unspecified jam and needed a sizeable amount of cash to tide him over a bridging arrangement. Frances, without telling Duncan, had offered to help and had insisted upon lending him the bulk of their savings in the certain belief of being repaid with interest within months. At this juncture she would lay emphasis on the moral debt they both felt they owed Bernard which, when all was said and done, was a point Duncan had never been slow to make himself. There had been some unforeseen delay but Bernard had promised restitution of the debt in good time for Duncan's release. Unluckily for everyone, he had been murdered before repayment could be made, and it now never would be.

She examined this hypothesis from all sides. It was the only possibility and had the added advantage of making Bernard's death the last contingency she or Alistair could desire. She would have to satisfy Duncan of its plausibility, also the police who would no doubt go through the books at Bruton and King with a fine-tooth comb. Her visit to that office could be explained by the Midas shares booming and her wanting to know by how much their small investment had increased in value. George had obviously never known the amount originally entrusted to Bernard for investment. She went over it again. It could hold water. It would have to. Was it only hours ago that she had held up her hands in holy horror at the idea of being a party to theft when here she was immersed in murder?

She thought about Alistair lying in the double bed at the club beside Amelia and wondered if he slept. His was the harder part to play, with no moment of privacy since the horror of the previous evening. To have taken such an insane risk he had been driven hard, bled silently for over thirteen years. A further thirteen might have been tolerated if she hadn't fallen in love with Bernard. It had been her confession which had pushed Alistair over the edge. Had he got back to the club safely? Had he kept his nerve? For all that she knew, now that he had implicated her, he might decide to give himself up. It would be in keeping with his outmoded sense of chivalry. He had protected Amelia all this time. She laid her head wearily back against the chair and almost wished he would. That way she'd be free and shot of them all. She had more than fulfilled her obligation to their family. What right had they to expect more? You had to think of yourself — take what you wanted. Bernard had taught her that. Bernard. He was what she wanted, nobody, nothing else. But he was dead.

Reasoning came to an abrupt halt. The significant finality of the fact spread along the numbed nerve endings of Frances's mind, which in turn sent their own messages into her physical parts. A dull soreness in the region of her heart spread downwards to her stomach in a reflex arc of pain, twisting her gut nauseously. Her chest was constricted in an aching rigidity as if all its muscles were contained in quick-setting cement. A rigor gripped her spine and she flexed her hands on the chair arms to control its symptoms. An animal somewhere was making a noise as if it were caught in a trap and Frances wished it would stop until she realized it was the sound of her own grief which would not be suppressed. Like a dry labour, it racked her until the flooding relief of tears surged painfully up through her strangulated throat, breaking down the dam of resistance. Abandoning herself to shock and despair, Frances cried shudderingly and noisily, the sobs wrenched from an inner void, reverberating through the top of her aching skull.

She didn't know how long she sat there, rocking backwards and forwards, deserted by control and calling Bernard's name futilely in her desolation. During intervals between the bouts of crying she would attempt to get a hold on herself, only to be reminded by her inward eye of his lifeless body as it had lain at Alistair's feet, and the realization of all that she had lost overcame her anew, quickening the tears. Whatever he was, she loved him, and he *had* loved her. That part of it had been true and good, whatever else was rotten. A moralist would say that there was precious little truth about marital infidelity or the betrayal of friendship, but if she couldn't believe that it had been special, what was left to her?

Gradually the paroxysms passed and Frances sat on, cold and shrivelled, tears drying stiffly on her face, eyes sore and pitted in her swollen cheeks, her head splitting across the crown and down the left facial nerves in a mammoth migraine. Eventually she summoned the strength to replenish the glass which stood on the table beside her from a half-depleted bottle of whisky which had been full the previous evening. She was drinking too much. No wonder she had such a hellish head. Dragging herself out of the chair, she stumbled away upstairs in search of aspirin. There were some in her dressing-table drawer and, collapsing on a stool, she shook a couple, then one more, into her palm and knocked them back with the rest of the spirit. Her ravaged face in the mirror, blotched, bloated and ugly with grief, brought her up short as the hand holding the glass was arrested on its downward journey. Falteringly the pathetic vision smoothed its flattened, salt-streaked hair and ran its fingertips over the contours of its face to reassure itself of its identity. So, she'd been reduced to this. Correction. She'd reduced herself to this. She couldn't blame anyone else. An early instinct had warned her against Bernard, but she had chosen to ignore it, had in fact courted disaster by encouraging and loving him. Even had he not died, she would have been crying now at the termination of their affair. At their last meeting he had revealed to her the true extent to which his mind was twisted. She couldn't have gone on with him, yet she doubted the strength of her determination to do without him, had he lived. Previously she'd never understood the complete subjugation of principle, duty and honour and trust to physical passion, but now in the cold dawn hours she was forced to admit that Alistair might have saved her from a fate worse than the death of her lover. In any case, there was no going back. The stirrings of her instinct for survival dictated the relegation of soul-searching, nostalgia and regrets. She had to live through tonight and tomorrow and all the endless succeeding days, one step at a time. She'd done it once before with Duncan. She could do it again. Resourceful Frances! The tower of strength! She smiled grimly, then shivered.

There was nothing like the comfort of a hot bath after alcoholically induced emotional dehydration. If she wound up her mind and set it along a purposeful track, in mundane action she could return to some semblance of normality. After she had soaked her exhausted, aching limbs and washed her hair, she lay on the bed and slipped into unconsciousness.

★ ★ ★

An hour later the Sunday-morning paper boy banged the flap on the letter-box and Frances was instantly awake. Seven o'clock. Exactly twelve hours ago Bernard had been kissing her for the last time. That way madness lay. Frances got up and dressed, making up her face and pulling the bedclothes together. She thought of how she had arranged the counterpane on Bernard's bed and the ecstasy that had been shared between those sheets. She found nothing in either of the papers, no reference to the discovery of a body or a burglar, although she combed the minutest print with diligence. They surely must have found him. Unless the alarm had not gone off after all. In that case Bernard could lie there until Monday morning when George would miss him from the office. Frances was unable to gauge whether such a contingency would be to hers and Alistair's advantage or not. Whatever the case, they could only stick to their stories as arranged. And she wished to Christ that Alistair would hurry up and get down here so that they *could* arrange between them what should be said. She hung about, frittering away time on trivial jobs that didn't require any concentration, afraid of going into the garden for fear of missing a vital phone call. Waiting undermined morale and she prayed that something, anything, would break today, but please God not before she had seen Alistair.

They arrived at last shortly before eleven-thirty and Frances was immensely relieved that Alistair looked much like himself and showed no visible signs of being under strain. She marvelled at his aptitude for covering up before she reminded herself that he had been playing a part certainly for as long as she had known him. You never knew what you might find under the skin if you scratched people. She thought of Bernard again.

'We're not stopping long, Frances.' Amelia kissed her lightly on both cheeks while Frances looked over her shoulder to encounter Alistair's eyes. He gave her a small reassuring nod, then came forward to greet her himself.

'All well, Frances?' He held her hands and exerted an extra pressure as he asked the question.

'Fine. And you?'

'Fine too.'

'Good.' Only he could interpret her smile as one of relief. 'This is a nice surprise. What brings you here?'

'Alistair was lecturing last night in town. We thought we'd call in on the way home. I told him it wasn't fair because I've got this streaming cold.' Amelia put a handkerchief to her nose and for the first time Frances noticed that she looked pinched and decidedly peaky.

'I'm sorry you have, but I'm glad you did. Have a nice hot cup of coffee.' Frances went into the kitchen and Alistair followed her.

'She's not really at all herself,' he confided, his brow creased with a worried frown. The sum total of his present troubles would appear to be Amelia's mild indisposition and Frances wondered if, like herself, the improbable equation of his everyday self with his dramatic role of the previous night was receding into fantasy.

'Sit her down and give her this.' She put a steaming cup into his hand. 'I'm going to make an excuse to take you into the garden.' Allowing him time to go through, she went to the door and said, 'Now that you're here, can you spare a moment and a word of advice about some cuttings I want to take? I know Alistair's the expert.'

Amelia, thankful not to have to leave her seat, sipped her coffee and watched her husband and Frances strolling companionably down the garden path. They stopped at intervals to inspect a plant, apparently deep in horticultural topics.

'You got back all right?'

'No trouble at all. I went in the side entrance — the ladies' door. Everyone was dressing for dinner. My mac was wet but

I accounted for that by dropping it in the shower. And you?'

'OK too. I thought of everything I could.' She told him in detail of her preparations and departure from the flat. 'I don't know if it worked. There's nothing in the paper.'

'We'll have to wait.'

'What about the cartridge case?'

'I'll get rid of it.'

'You must. That's all-important. I sat up all night thinking about the money.' She bent to a mallow plant and showed him the new growth on the old wood. 'This is what we must say.' She outlined her plan. 'I couldn't think of another explanation that wouldn't lead them to us.'

He nodded and brought his head down to hers to inspect the flower.

'Sounds all right as far as it goes. They'll ferret to find out what he wanted the money for.'

She laughed up at him. Amelia, the onlooker, petulantly envied them their shared amusement.

'Blackmail?' she suggested. 'After all, he was a queer, wasn't he?'

There was a gleam of admiration in his eyes.

She went on, 'You mustn't be the one to mention that. Better the merest hint from me, then if they ask you, you can back me up. And I'll be the one to break the news to Duncan.'

His face clouded. 'I feel so guilty, Frances. Not about Bernard, but about you. I thought all night too. The fairest thing would be for me to give myself up.' Unconsciously he looked towards the house from which Amelia watched. The glance spoke volumes and she knew that they were only token words. As long as she lived he would make live sacrifices to Amelia. He saw the look on her face. 'Why should I expect you to incriminate yourself?'

'I'm already in up to my neck.'

'I could say I had done it.'

'But you won't, will you?'

'No.' He looked down at the ground. 'I'm sorry, but no. Not as long as I believe we can get away with it. That bastard had thirteen years of my life. He's not getting the rest of it if I can help it. I couldn't know you would be there.'

'Seemingly it was just as well that I was.' She couldn't prevent a touch of asperity.

The look he gave her was tinged with shame. 'I have no right to put you through this.'

She was reminded of when Duncan had said he would understand if she didn't stick by him. Neither of them meant it. They both took her reliability for granted. No useful purpose could be served in Alistair's surrender of himself, merely additional notoriety and the further devastation of all their lives. Bernard had to be denied that final victory. Nevertheless Frances grappled momentarily with an ignoble sense of martyrdom.

Amelia, calling from the window 'Frances! Telephone!' interrupted them and recalled Frances to the immediate necessity for watching and weighing words and movements from now on. It had started. Without knowing who was on the other end of the line, she was sure of that.

'Remember. Stick to what we agreed. I rely on you as much as you do on me. No misplaced heroics.' She left him to follow at his own pace as she hurried into the house.

# 16

George Bruton's voice came as a surprise.

'Is that you, Mrs Parry?'

'Yes. Mr Bruton? What can I do for you on a Sunday?'

'I'm afraid I have some very bad news concerning Mr King, Mrs Parry. The police came to see me early this morning. They didn't know who else to contact — Mr King having no close relatives. He was attacked during a burglary at his flat last night and shot. Shot dead, that is,' he added, aware that he'd been circumlocutory.

'Dead!' Frances's voice was suitably unbelieving and hollow.

'I'm afraid so. I can't take it in either.'

'But — how did it happen? And when?' She knew the answer to the first question, but hung expectantly upon the second.

'It seems that somebody broke in when Mr King was upstairs and he came down and was shot in the commotion. Round about eight o'clock, I believe.'

'Commotion?'

'Apparently the burglar alarm had been tripped off — that's what took the police

248

there. Otherwise he might have lain there for hours or even days. The place had been turned over.'

'Oh my God!' Frances sat down. She didn't have to feign weakness. Bile rose in her throat and her knees were shaking. Alistair came into the hall and looked as if he were about to ask her something, but she restrained him with her hand and he remained there listening to her side of the interchange. Amelia, who had caught odd words and realized some drama was afoot, stood behind him in the doorway.

'Are you all right?' George's voice was anxious.

'Yes — but — Oh, God, what a ghastly thing!'

'I'm sorry to be the one to have to break the news, but I thought it better coming from me than from the police. I asked them if I could. They're on their way to see you now. I gave them your address and that of Sir Alistair, seeing that you were all Mr King's closest friends.'

'Yes, of course, and thank you.' She hadn't thought about who they would contact first. Bernard had no relatives. They hadn't been slow in getting around to George. 'How did they find you on a Sunday?' she asked.

'There were the firm's cards in Mr King's

wallet, and my home address in his diary,' George explained. 'In the absence of any next of kin they asked me if I would identify the body. I took the liberty. I hope that was all right.' He sounded tentative, afraid of being accused of usurping her own prerogative. It was one contingency she had overlooked and Frances was thankful that neither she nor Alistair had been required to fulfil this duty.

'That was very good of you,' she said unsteadily.

There was a pause, then George said, 'He looked very peaceful. There was nothing to show.' He was reassuring her that Bernard's brains hadn't been blown out, and a part of her registered gratitude. Another part remembered the neat black hole and the spreading bloodstain. The silence stretched out. 'Are you there, Mrs Parry?'

'Yes. I'm sorry. I was thinking. Thank you so much for all you've done, Mr Bruton. It must have all been extremely unpleasant for you. I can't seem to take it in.'

'It's hard, I know. One reads about these things — all too common these days — thugs and vandals — but somehow when it strikes home — ' His voice trembled and Frances suffered a pang of added remorse for George's steadfast loyalty. She could imagine him removing his glasses and wiping them with controlled emotion. 'If I can be of any assistance, no matter how great or small, you know you can call upon me, Mrs Parry. Perhaps you would be kind enough to let me know what arrangements have been made about the funeral eventually.'

'Of course. I suppose the police didn't say how long it would be before they'd release the — ' She hesitated over the word 'body'.

George cleared his throat discreetly. 'I didn't ask. No doubt they'll tell you themselves.'

★ ★ ★

She remembered he'd said that they were on their way. The imminence of their arrival provoked a sense of panic which had to be swallowed as she concluded the exchange with George with additional thanks and commiserations. As Frances replaced the receiver Amelia could no longer be restrained.

'What is it? What's happened?' Her white face, sharp with alarm, blanched to a shade of grey as Frances relayed the news, and she turned instinctively to catch at Alistair's coat sleeve for support in her appalled shock and

251

grief. He was there. Frances watched him gently enfold her within his arm and propel her back into the sitting-room and towards a chair. His completely genuine concern for her distress tided him over the dangerous moment when histrionics could normally have been expected of him, and Amelia, as usual absorbed in her own reactions, had no consideration for her husband's response to the news, which was just as well. When he looked up and asked Frances if she had any brandy, their eyes met and reaffirmed their resolution. Fortified by that look, Frances went to get the bottle and poured two decorous glasses which she carried through to Alistair and Amelia, giving him the smaller amount. He'd need all his wits about him. So would she.

Her mind ran swiftly over the details. Had anything been overlooked? With scant moments to go before the arrival of their visitors, Frances suddenly thought of Bernard's keys. They were still in her handbag. She had asked Alistair about the disposal of the cartridge case but she had clean forgotten her own rubbish. The duster and the rubber gloves reposed innocently enough in her kitchen drawer, but the keys mustn't be found on these premises. Making an excuse to go upstairs, she raced up and extracted the offending articles from her purse and debated what to do with them. Found anywhere at No. 6 they were incriminating, but there was now no time to take them further afield. There were two of them, a small Yale and a longer brass Chubb. On a hasty decision, Frances unbuttoned her blouse and slipped them down into the front of her bra. Better on her until she could get rid of them. She couldn't believe the police's initial visit would involve a personal search. She arranged her clothes and closed her bag as she heard the approach of cars, followed by the slamming of doors. She went slowly downstairs.

★ ★ ★

Detective-Inspector Walter was a spare, ferret-faced man with sandy brows and hair and a pointed nose and chin that jutted forward inquisitively. His pale blue eyes darted in nervous fashion between the assembled company, although of them all he was the least likely to be suffering from any lack of confidence. His side-kick, a sergeant in plain clothes, was a plump, smooth-skinned young man with broad wet lips and a merry expression incongruous upon one bringing intelligence of horror and sudden death. Bob Lawton stood respectfully beside his superior, awaiting instructions.

'Won't you sit down, Inspector?' Frances indicated the two upright chairs flanking the D-end table. 'I don't know whether you need something to write on.'

Walter thanked her and motioned to Lawton to be seated, while Frances and Amelia assumed the armchairs and Alistair remained standing between them, his back to the fireplace. Upon introduction to Duncan's parents, Bob Lawton had narrowly restrained himself from commenting upon the fortuity of killing two birds with one stone, smiling inwardly as he contemplated the birds in question. The old girl reminded him of a peacock, displayed in bright colours and preening to restore her equanimity before strangers. Sir Alistair — more like an eagle — protective wingspan, noble head, intent expression, patrician beaky nose. Both of the old school. Stiff upper lips and family escutcheons. The young one was a corker. It was all there but it wasn't thrown at you. Sexy with class, and brains. His lip glistened and he turned his attention to what Walter, who was addressing himself to Frances, was saying.

'This is very tragic for you all, Mrs Parry. I realize that. Mr Bruton tells me that Mr King is as one of the family — was, that is.'

Frances nodded.

'How was that?'

'His parents were dead. Originally they were missionaries abroad so Mr King had no relatives in England. He became friendly with my husband when they were at school and Sir Alistair and Lady Parry befriended him.'

'He was like a second son to us,' Amelia said, her voice breaking on the words.

'I see.' Walter made a note. 'So you know of no relative — distant or otherwise — here or abroad?'

'There were none,' Alistair said.

'Thank you, sir. Friends?'

'I don't know a lot about Bernard's social habits. You and Duncan would know more about that.' Alistair turned to Frances, who racked her brain and came up with a couple of names of people met at distant dinner-parties in Brandon Court. 'He never talked about any close friendships,' she concluded.

'It doesn't matter too much. We have his diary. There are names and addresses in that. We shall be following them up. What about enemies?'

Walter watched their blank expressions. Frances willed herself to look sorrowfully straight at him, her brows creased in a suggestion of bewilderment.

'Not that I know of,' she said.

255

Alistair shrugged and said 'Sorry', while Amelia opined that she couldn't imagine Bernard having an enemy in the world.

'We have to cover every possibility, madam. It will all have to be gone into in more detail later, but anything that you can think of could be helpful. Just as I now have to ask the three of you where you were at eight o'clock last night.' He looked enquiringly at Alistair, waiting for him to volunteer.

'Certainly.' Alistair's voice was just right, courteous and helpful without being too pat or ingratiating. 'My wife and I stayed in town last night at my club.' He supplied its name and location. 'We were guests of honour at a dinner at the Trafalgar rooms where I delivered a lecture on the openings for youth in various industries. Dinner was timed for eight-thirty. Drinks beforehand, seven forty-five. My wife and I had been asked to make a point of being punctual. There were a great many people to meet — captains of industry and the like.' He watched the bowed heads of both policemen, mentally on tiptoe for the next question. His answer appeared to satisfy Walter. The ferret profile swivelled in Frances's direction.

'And you, madam?'

'I had supper with my sister, Dolly Moodie. She lives in a flat in Richmond a couple of miles away. We do turn and turn about alternate Saturdays. I arrived about eight. A little before, I think, because she commented on my being early.' He hadn't asked her if she'd gone straight there. It had been dark and wet when she had taken the car out of the garage at six o'clock and the road had been empty. There was another bit of luck she'd have to trust to. The pale blue eyes skewered her and she began to realize that Detective-Inspector Walter was not as insignificant as his appearance suggested.

'Did your husband accompany you?'

'My husband?' It wasn't the question she had anticipated and she faltered.

'You are married to Sir Alistair's son — Mr King's great friend?' His eyes travelled past her to the wedding photograph on the mantelpiece. Frances felt sure those eyes could turn corners. She was almost ready to believe they could detect the two keys lying under her breasts.

'My husband is away serving a term of imprisonment in Sussex. He's to be released in three weeks' time.' If it was news to him Walter evinced no surprise. She leaned forward. 'That's something I would like to ask, Inspector. Would it be possible for me to break this ghastly thing to him personally? He thought the world of Mr King. It's going to be a very bad shock for him. I don't want him to read about it in the papers or to be told by strangers.'

A suspicion of humanity relaxed the Inspector's weaselly mouth. 'I think that could be arranged. We'll be wanting a statement from him in any case. Sergeant Lawton could go with you.'

'But my husband couldn't possibly be able to tell you anything about Mr King's death.'

Walter regarded her blandly. 'Just a formality, madam.'

Alistair intervened. 'What actually did happen, Inspector? George Bruton told my daughter-in-law that Mr King had been shot. How and why?'

'That's what we're trying to find out, sir. How is simple. Mr King was shot in the chest with a nine-millimetre bullet from an automatic weapon. We recovered the bullet from the wood panelling to the right of the door. Why? It would appear that Mr King disturbed a burglar who shot him in panic before escaping. Mr King was apparently quite a collector — a connoisseur. By the way, Mrs Parry, are you familiar with the contents of Mr King's apartment?'

If you weren't attending you could easily be confused by the way he threw out these sudden little trip wires. Frances was glad she had resisted the brandy.

'I've been there quite a bit — social occasions with my husband. I know the lie of the land,' she said.

'Would you be in a position to tell us whether anything had been taken or was missing?'

'I don't know. I might. There are certain ornaments and things I remember, but I couldn't swear to be accurate.'

'What about you, sir, and Lady Parry?'

'We'd never been to Bernard's flat, had we, Alistair?' Amelia looked up at her husband for confirmation. 'Bernard always used to come down to Falconers.' The remembrance of those visits caused her delicately to wipe the corner of her eye. There had been no public tears for Duncan, Frances reflected somewhat bitterly.

Walter shook his head. 'A pity. Mr Bruton evidently has no knowledge of it either. In the circumstances, Mrs Parry, I shall have to ask you if you would come with me to Mr King's flat where you might be able to assist us in discovering whether the thief took anything traceable.'

'Now?' Frances was visibly disturbed. She hadn't expected or desired ever to set foot in Brandon Court again as long as she lived.

The memory of how she had left it was sufficiently ineradicable to haunt her for the rest of her days and now she was being asked to go back and relive the scene under the gimlet eyes of Detective-Inspector Walter. It would require a cooler nerve than she possessed at the moment. Perhaps he already suspected her and this suggestion was some kind of a trap. She took a grip on her runaway imagination. There were steps to take, moves to be made, intelligently, like a game.

'Not this moment. Perhaps a little later today. I appreciate your first anxiety is to break this sad news to your husband. I suggest that, at your convenience, Sergeant Lawton conveys you to Sussex, after which he can return you to London, say near enough four o'clock, when we can meet at Brandon Court. It won't take long, and he can bring you home.'

'Thank you.' Nobody said anything, so Frances stood up uncertainly. Walter and Lawton snapped their notebooks shut and rose in unison.

Alistair asked, 'Have you finished with us, Inspector? I'd like to get my wife home.'

'Yes, thank you, sir.'

'We'll be going then, Frances. Goodbye, my dear.' He embraced her, and the message communicated by the pressure of his hands upon her upper arms imbued her with courage. The policemen remained in the drawing-room as Frances saw her in-laws out. On her return they were conferring in lowered voices which halted on her entry.

'What about the prison? Should somebody ring them?'

'No need. Sergeant Lawton will see about the formalities when you get there.'

Frances looked from one to the other. 'I'll just get ready, then.'

As she gathered her things and took a coat out of the wardrobe she stood for a second preparing herself for the all-important interview with her husband. Husband! The title had a false ring. Bernard should have been her husband. She couldn't have felt more completely widowed and alone.

# 17

Frances waited for Duncan in a small office two doors down from the recreation room where they usually met. She had been ushered into it while Sergeant Lawton explained the nature of their mission to the prison authorities, and now she stood looking out of the window, listening for his returning footsteps. When she heard them, she braced her shoulders and turned to face the door.

★ ★ ★

Duncan's expression was a mixture of surprise and anxiety as he entered the room and saw her. 'Frances! They said someone to see me, but not who.' He kissed her on her cheek, noticing her stance and how pale she was. 'Is something wrong?'

'I'll wait outside.' Bob Lawton in the open door withdrew, closing it behind him. They were alone but the room might be bugged. The sheer melodrama of the past twenty-four hours stimulated suspicions that would have been absurd two days ago.

'Something *is* wrong,' Duncan insisted. 'What is it?'

'I'm afraid so. Darling, Bernard is dead.'

Duncan stared at her and she nodded her head gently to reaffirm her words. 'He died last night.'

He lowered himself slowly on to the office chair and Frances leaned back against the desk for support. 'But how? An accident?'

'Sort of. He was shot in his flat. A burglar got in and Bernard surprised him. He was armed.'

'Murder?'

Frances nodded again. 'It looks that way.'

'Dear God!' He was silent, taking it in, then he said again, 'Dear God! Bernard.'

'I know.' Frances put out her hand to touch him in a gesture of comfort but found that she couldn't, so withdrew it.

Presently he said, 'What a senseless way for a person like Bernard to go. Have they got the man?'

'Not yet. It's more difficult when it's a random killing.'

He looked up at her, his eyes dark with pain. 'Was it instantaneous, Fran?'

'I think so. From what George said.'

'George?'

'He identified the body.' Frances told him of George's part in the affair and of his phone call. Her voice was flat and expressionless, her mind picking only those facts she had heard either from George or the police. It would be too easy to slip in some extraneous piece of description deriving from her personal knowledge of the event.

'What a terrible thing. Bernard of all people.' Duncan covered his eyes with his hand and when he took it away it was wet with the tears that stained his cheeks. He said pathetically, 'He was my best friend, Fran. What am I going to do without him?'

Frances clenched her hands on the strap of her handbag. 'We'll have to manage somehow. It's going to be even more difficult than you imagine. There's more bad news connected with his death. Do you want to hear the rest?'

'More?'

She pitied him. He looked as though he didn't believe life could hold any worse, but time was short and it all had to be said. She moved round to assume the seat on the other side of the desk. It was the only other chair in the room and, sitting in it, too late she realized she had adopted what Duncan could misinterpret as the managerial stance.

'Yes. I hardly know where to start. I wish you'd told me earlier, Duncan, about your idea of buying up this business in

Basingstoke. It came as a bolt out of the blue when your father came and said things had moved as far and as fast as they had, that you wanted to sell the Midas shares. Actually Alistair took me down to Basingstoke last week and I saw for myself the possibilities there. As it happened, I should have encouraged you in any other circumstances. What hurt was that you evidently didn't think I would.'

Duncan looked sheepish. To save himself from explanation he said, with a hint of truculence, 'What's all that got to do with Bernard?'

She drew in her breath and fiddled with a pencil on the blotter in front of her. 'Only that there aren't any shares — Midas or otherwise — at least nothing like the number on Bernard's list. The money from Hill House was never invested. Not the bulk.'

His expression was now one of bewilderment. 'What in God's name happened to it, then?'

'I lent it to Bernard.'

'You what?'

'I lent it to Bernard. Just after you came here and the house was sold, Bernard told me he was in some kind of a jam. He needed ready cash and, I gathered, quickly. It was to be a short-term loan — no question about us getting it back, and because I was in a position to help him out, I did what I thought you would have done yourself. There was some delay with the various transactions he was making, but he was on the point of repaying the money with interest this week. Now he's dead.'

'Are you seriously telling me that over £200,000 of ours has gone down the drain?' His face was white but he spoke quietly and rationally.

'I'm saying there's not much left of the original £150,000. There would have been nothing like £200,000 without the Midas boom. That might not have happened. I couldn't be expected to have foreseen that.'

'But it *did* happen, Fran. And I was kept under the impression we had those investments. Why was I kept in the dark? It was my money, after all.'

'I'm sorry. It seemed best at the time not to bother you.' It sounded thin so she embroidered. 'Bernard had to be persuaded to take the loan. He wasn't too proud of himself. If Midas hadn't boomed and Bernard hadn't by a hundred to one chance been killed, you wouldn't have known anything about it — wouldn't have been out of pocket. As it is — everything's gone wrong.'

Duncan stood up suddenly and leaned

towards her over the desk. 'And you accuse me of not taking you into my confidence! That's what hurt you! Jesus, Fran, you're too much. I suppose you thought you'd tell me what was good for me. Organize my money in the same way you always organized me. You even gave me all that crap about following the stock market. You're a consummate actress. I'll give you that.'

'I thought you'd want to help your friend. God knows you owed him,' Frances said coldly.

'I hardly need you to remind me of that.'

'What would you have done, then?'

'Probably exactly the same as you, but I had a right to know. I've gone ahead and made plans. Now they're all up the creek.'

'If you'd told me about those plans as well as your father, I could have prevented your hopes being raised.' It was providential that he hadn't or Frances wouldn't be able to get away with this lie now.

'And do you know why I didn't?' He thrust his face close up to hers. 'Just for once I wanted to make a decision of my own to prove that I was master of my fate. I knew that you would oppose the idea, Frances. It wasn't yours. You'd prefer to have me safely under your thumb working for you — the husband of Mrs Frances Parry.'

She said stiffly, 'I'm sorry you've been disappointed but it's not as if I deliberately threw your money down the drain. Blame Bernard if you have to blame somebody.'

'That's not in very good taste, Fran.'

'No. I'm sorry.' She was sourly amused by his reprimand. She felt like screaming 'Blame Bernard for the whole bloody shambles of your father, your marriage and your future! Blame your sainted friend for being the balls-aching bastard of all time!' Denying herself that satisfaction, she remained silent, ostensibly suitably chastened.

He relaxed his attitude and dropped back again into his chair spiritlessly. 'I don't understand why Bernard should need money — and from us. His credit was good and he had the appearance of affluence. If things had been really tight he could have sold something. He wasn't short of a crust.' It was a valid question and one for which Frances had a ready answer for the police, but not yet for Duncan.

She said, 'I wondered — but I didn't ask. Bernard didn't stop to ask questions, did he? I could only remember that.' It was worthy of the script of the corniest soap opera but Duncan was unaware of any hypocrisy.

'It's surely a terrible blow. Terrible.' Once again he put his head in his hands and

Frances couldn't tell whether he meant the loss of the money or Bernard's demise was the worse catastrophe.

She looked at her watch. 'Sergeant Lawton wants to have a word with you before we go.'

'What for?' He looked up, alarmed.

'Only to ask you anything you knew about Bernard's habits, I expect. He kept pretty much to himself and the smallest clue could help. You can probably remember better than I some of the things he had in his flat. Detective-Inspector Walter wants me to look over it to see if anything's missing, but I don't know it that well.'

For the first time he considered her. 'This has been pretty terrible for you, Fran. I'm sorry I was aggressive.'

'That's all right.' She smiled tightly. 'It couldn't matter less.' Nor could it — nor could he, she was shocked to discover. 'Don't worry about the future. We'll work something out.'

A curious expression shadowed his eyes before he dropped them. She had a feeling that he had nearly said something but had decided to keep it back. He grasped her hand. 'Will you do something? Will you find out exactly what I'm — what we're worth — apart from your business?'

'I'll do that.'

They stood awkwardly, confronting each other, both reticent of making physical contact. Providentially, at that moment Bob Lawton broke in upon their stilted exchange giving Frances the excuse to make her adieux and escape, leaving the two men to their interview.

★ ★ ★

She got into the empty police car and sat there while her pulse rate regulated and the sweat dried beneath the hairline on her neck. It had been an ordeal, but there was worse to come. Detective-Inspector Walter was not a man to be easily manipulated. The clock dial on the dashboard registered just after two o'clock and Frances's stomach reminded her that she hadn't eaten since the night before. She had been too hung over and jaded for breakfast and too taut and nervous to grab a snack before setting off with Sergeant Lawton. She'd not been at her best with Duncan, breaking the news baldly, even coldly, and wanting to get it over before either she gave herself away or the numbness that had replaced her total disintegration of the previous night thawed, rendering her incapable of intrigue.

'Sorry to keep you.' Sergeant Lawton was back, swinging himself easily into the driving seat and snapping his seat-belt into place. 'Everything all right?' He scrutinized her pale face with a friendly, anxious expression and Frances warmed to his concern.

'He was pretty shattered,' she said. 'There's no way to wrap that sort of news up. I hope I wasn't too clumsy but there was the time factor.'

'I hope you didn't feel rushed. I could have waited longer,' he said politely.

'No. No, we'd really said it all.' She wondered what questions he had asked Duncan and whether the latter had mentioned the money.

Lawton started the car and reversed out of the parking bay. 'I expect you could do with some food. We'll stop somewhere for a sandwich. Will that do you?'

'I am hungry,' she admitted.

When he said he knew of a place Frances prayed that it wouldn't be the same one Bernard and she had made their own, but of course that would have been a chance in a million, and anyway, she'd forgotten that mercifully they'd be turning off to take the London road before they came to 'their' pub.

Bob Lawton's 'place' was a lorry-drivers'

pull-in where he demolished a plate of egg and chips and Frances downed a couple of toasted sandwiches and two mugs full of restoratively strong tea. When they had finished there was more colour in her cheeks and the dangerous mental lassitude that had threatened clear thinking had receded.

'I'll meet you outside,' she said, pushing back her chair and picking up her handbag. 'See you in the car.' Leaving him to pay the bill, her share of which she had offered but had been refused, she went out into the car park. The lay-by in which the café stood backed on to a field which was in the process of being cleared by bulldozers for the extension of the dual carriageway. On their arrival Frances had registered the presence of a large skip filled with slate, sand and builders' rubble standing a short distance away from two doors which advertised facilities for 'Ladies' and 'Gents'. All the workmen were on the far side of the field and there was no one to witness her from any of the cars as she moved swiftly across to the skip. Delving into her cleavage, she extricated the keys, then dropped them over the side of the container into the debris, nipping smartly into the loo to emerge some minutes later to find her escort awaiting her.

They hardly spoke all the way to London.

At his suggestion, Frances sat in the back of the car and found it easier to feign sleep than to sustain the sporadic conversation necessary had she kept her eyes open. She was summoning her strength and her wits for Inspector Walter and her enforced return to the scene of the crime. Life was a series of clichés rendering the most devastating of its moments banal. They said all criminals were compulsively drawn back. Opening her eyes, she saw her face reflected in the windscreen mirror. It looked perfectly ordinary. 'There's no art to find the mind's construction in the face.' They were words spoken by another Duncan. She'd done *Macbeth* at school. She'd never been much of an actress and had only had a small role. Closing her lids, mentally she rehearsed her forthcoming performance.

# 18

There was a policeman on the pavement outside the house in Brandon Court and two cars drawn up by the kerb. Lawton parked his behind them, then got out and came round to open Frances's door. She followed him up the steps and into the lobby where he rested his thumb against the lift button and they both waited for the elevator to come to rest and its doors to admit them.

'We're early but the boss is here,' he said conversationally on the way up.

On the third-floor landing Bernard's door stood ajar. They crossed the width of the carpet and Lawton preceded her into the flat. All the doors to the rooms were open and Frances managed to restrain her first glance from going to the spot on the floor where Bernard had lain. Instead she was able to meet Inspector Walter's eyes on their own level as he materialized from the drawing-room on Lawton's tentative call of 'Sir!'

'Ah! Mrs Parry. Mission concluded successfully?'

'Yes, thank you.'

'Good. How did your husband take it?'

'Like us all. Pretty stunned.'

'Yes, well, I apologize for having to put you through this further ordeal. Let's hope it won't take long. We'd better start in here.' He beckoned her and Frances managed to walk into the room without hesitation or lowering her gaze.

Everything was in the same shambles in which she had left it and nothing appeared to have been touched, except that all Bernard's lovingly polished antiques bore traces of grey, tacky fingerprint powder. There was another difference, one which her eye registered immediately as it traversed the room and she allowed it to encompass the sculpture, and move on. The plug of the contraption had been pulled out of its socket and lay on the floor. Conscious of the watchful gaze of the ferret, she allowed a not altogether simulated tremor to pass through her before she turned to him and said, 'My God! What a ghastly mess!'

'Not as bad as some we have to deal with in terms of filth. This bloke was a specialist. He knew what he was after and whatever his speciality there was plenty of potential here. Now, Mrs Parry, what I want you to do is to have a good look around, without touching anything, and see if you can notice anything missing.'

Frances nodded, and he stood in the middle of the room, his hands in his pockets, as she pretended to do a minute tour of inspection, pausing in front of the display cabinets to note their contents, mentally marking the furniture and checking on the pistol collection. The glass from the broken window still lay on the carpet.

'Is this where he got in?'

'It would seem so, madam.'

'I see.' She looked from the window back to Walter. 'Can you please tell me where exactly it happened, Inspector?'

He moved across to the door and stood facing her. 'About here. Mr King was facing him. He was shot at fairly close range. One bullet.'

Frances looked down at the place where his feet were firmly planted and thought of the hole that the bullet had made.

'Of course we're searching for the weapon now. Whoever he was, he was cool-headed enough to remember to pocket the cartridge case in all the hullabaloo.' He could see that he had puzzled her, so he elaborated. 'You'd normally expect to find a cartridge case from an automatic round. It would have been ejected probably about here.' He took a few paces forward. 'To the right if the bloke had been right-handed, or to the left if he was left-handed. He wasn't taking any chances. More difficult to prove what gun was used without the case.'

'I see.' She smiled faintly. 'Ironic, really. If only he had known, there was a selection of weapons already to hand here.'

His eyes went past her to the wall and Frances held her breath, wondering if she'd overplayed her hand.

'None of those would fire an automatic round. Need a powder horn for most of them. Actually it *is* feasible to use such a bullet in that type of thing.' He pointed to the Smith and Wesson whose handle and chamber were smudged with the ubiquitous grey dust, the sight of which had provoked her to gamble. 'It requires a certain amount of juggling. If it was used, then that would point to someone intimate enough with Mr King to know of its existence. Even allowing for that fact, they'd have to have been quick enough to enter, turn the place over, fiddle a cartridge into the breech, shoot Mr King, remove the case, clean the gun and replace it and get out of here and away within six minutes. I would say it was unlikely in the extreme, wouldn't you?'

'I don't know anything about ballistics, Inspector.'

'It would have taken nerve to stick around

once the alarm was set off and that went at — ' he consulted a small notebook — 'seven fifty-six.' He snapped a rubber band around the book and returned it to his pocket, still considering her. 'That's another thing that puzzles me, Mrs Parry. The alarm.'

On its way up to her mouth Frances's heart threatened to choke her half-way up her throat. Not trusting her voice to get past it, she continued to look at him enquiringly.

'Why should the alarm go off when Mr King was himself in the apartment?'

She swallowed the obstruction with relief. 'That's easily explained, Inspector. Mr King always set the downstairs circuit when he retired at night. The alarm is on two rings — up and down. You can set one or both.'

There was a stiffening of the probing thrust of his features as if the weasel scented prey. 'You are after all familiar with Mr King's habits, Mrs Parry? More familiar than you said at first?'

It was a shame to disappoint him. 'I happen to know about that particular habit, Inspector, because he told me himself when he explained to me how the alarm worked. I was thinking about having a similar system installed at my business. We discussed the workings of this one and he said then it was an advantage to have the two sets of switches because he always set the lower one at night.' She tried him further. 'But, Inspector, eight o'clock in the evening is hardly night time.'

'Mr King had evidently decided to have an early night. He had recently bathed and had his papers with him upstairs. He was in fact wearing only a bath robe when the shooting occurred.'

Frances accepted this information without comment. It was time to move him on. She said, 'I knew he'd been away all week. I tried to get him urgently on the Monday and spoke to him briefly, but he was on the point of setting off.'

The pink nose quivered. 'Something important?'

'Well, it was something that had cropped up unexpectedly. It's rather a long story.' She looked around her. 'Do you think we could sit down?'

He was at once all apologies and she subsided into a chair while he perched, alert and awkward-looking, on the edge of the sofa.

'When my husband went to prison I sold our house and it was agreed that the money be put into investments with Mr King dealing with all that side of it. That was my husband's wish. At about that time Mr King came to me and told me that he needed a sum in cash to tide him over some temporary trouble and I naturally offered to lend him what he needed. He was to repay it with interest and so long as I had it back by the time my husband was released it didn't matter to me whether it was earning interest in shares or with Mr King.'

'Naturally?'

Frances blinked. 'I beg your pardon?'

'You said you 'naturally' lent the money to Mr King.'

'Of course. He was a very old friend of my husband. More like a brother, but Lady Parry told you that.'

'You had no hesitation? You trusted him?'

'Implicitly.' She managed to convey shock that this should be in doubt and allowed a moment for this impression to sink in before continuing. 'I'm afraid I made an error of judgement at the time in not telling my husband what I had done.'

'Was that because you were afraid it might not appear so 'natural' to him?'

She didn't much like the sardonic emphasis on the word. 'No. In normal circumstances he would of course have been in agreement, but, Inspector, his circumstances at that moment were far from normal. His conviction and debarment from his profession had had a devastating effect upon his morale, and that was all he could think of or cope with. He was terribly depressed and I saw it as my duty to save him from any added pressures. Rightly or wrongly I took them upon myself. It seemed best. I was fairly independent financially. I have my own business, as I told you. My husband was under the impression that some shares, of which we do have a small holding — but he believed it to be substantially larger — due to a recent boom would finance him in a new venture on his release. As well as having to tell him of Mr King's death today, I had to disabuse him of this idea and tell him why. Mr King was due to repay the money this week. Once I knew what my husband was planning, I naturally wanted to speak to Mr King about it.' That word kept cropping up when there was nothing 'natural' about any of it.

'How did he take it?'

Frances made a little moue. 'As one would expect. Distraught about Mr King. Furious with me — not for lending the money, he admitted he would have done the same — but for not telling him. He resented my managerial ways.'

Walter said quietly, 'I imagine you've needed to know how to look after yourself.

281

Mr Bruton said you visited his offices on Friday. Was that in the hope of seeing Mr King?'

'I wondered if he might be back but he wasn't. We had discussed selling what few Midas shares we had and I wanted to see my portfolio and judge how much could be scraped together for my husband's venture. There wouldn't be as much as he expected, but with Mr King's repayment there might have been enough to make a start.'

Walter blew his nose and studiously cleaned each nostril. Replacing his handkerchief, he said, 'So as far as you were concerned, Mrs Parry, Mr King chose an inauspicious moment to die?'

'You could say that. Not that he had any choice in the matter. Poor Bernard.' Her voice was husky.

Walter got up and walked about the room, then turned back towards her. 'Have you any idea, Mrs Parry, what Mr King wanted that loan for?'

'None. He didn't say.'

'Was it for his business?'

'You'd have to ask Mr Bruton that.'

'From these surroundings one would say he was a gentleman of taste and even wealth.'

'He certainly never gave any appearance

of being hard up,' Frances agreed.

'You never asked him?'

'No, Inspector.'

He stood musing, testing his weight on the balls of his feet. 'What about his other friends?'

'I told you, Inspector. We only knew a couple of them very casually. He didn't speak of others.'

'And he was never married?'

'No.' She held her neck and stomach muscles rigid — waiting.

'But he had girl-friends — women?'

'No.' She shook her head. She could tell by the pregnant hesitation before he put his next question that her precision had not been lost upon him.

'How are you so sure about that when you say you know nothing of his friends?'

She allowed herself to appear embarrassed. 'I just know that Mr King was not interested in woman-friends.' Her eyes concentrated upon her hands in her lap, but she could sense the avidity with which his mind clamped on to her latent qualification.

'What are you trying to say, Mrs Parry?'

'Nothing.' She twisted her fingers. 'I just meant Mr King was not a woman's man.'

'Was he a man's man?'

She looked up at him as if relieved to be

offered the equivocation.

'He got on better with men.'

'You know I don't mean that. Was Mr King a homosexual?'

Frances said nothing, but her attitude and the silence spoke volumes.

'Well, was he?'

'I don't know, Inspector.'

'I think you do.' The pink nose twitched hungrily. It was feeding time.

She spoke falteringly. 'I really don't know for certain. I've accepted the possibility because of something my husband told me a long time ago. Apparently Mr King had a homosexual relationship with another young man when he was at Cambridge. He was sent down. My mother and father-in-law were particularly kind to him at that time. It's all water under the bridge. I don't see what bearing it could have upon all this.'

'It could have a significant bearing, Mrs Parry. If Mr King was a homosexual that opens the field for a variety of motives. Thank you for telling me what you have.'

Frances said modestly, 'I want to help. I don't think, though, that I could swear to anything either having or not having been taken from this room, Inspector.' She got up and took a last look round.

'You've been of great assistance. I'll find

Sergeant Lawton and get him to drive you home.' Walter went out into the hall and called his sergeant's name. When there was no reply he came back into the drawing-room.

'He's probably down with the car.' He crossed to the window with Frances in his wake and, kneeling on the window-sill, pressed his face to the pane to look into the street. His right foot was inches from the sculpture. It was a God-sent opportunity and instinct compelled Frances to act without a second's hesitation. As Walter shifted his position to rap on the window-pane, she bent swiftly, using her hand to sweep the sculpture forcibly off the edge of the window-seat in a shattering tinkling of glass. By the time he turned, aghast and annoyed, to see what he had dislodged she was standing three feet back surveying the damage, equally horrified. Part of the pillar had broken away from the base and two of the arms had snapped. The force of her blow had ensured that the branches had been dashed against the skirting-board where the broken-off pieces of metal lay among smashed green glass. With any luck it was beyond repair.

'Damn! That was clumsy.' He bent down to salvage it but Frances already had what was left of the sculpture in her hands. She set it carefully on the table. 'I can't think how it happened. Anyway, no good crying over spilt milk. Do you reckon it was valuable?' He peered at it closely.

'I believe so,' Frances said. 'An artistic protégé of Mr King's made it.'

'Can't see anything in modern art myself.' Walter's tone was derisory. 'Who made it, do you say?'

'I don't know him. He has a business in the Bayswater Road.'

'I suppose it meant something to him,' said the Inspector dubiously.

'I suppose so.'

'Oh, by the way, Mrs Parry, did you or your husband happen to have a key to this apartment, or can you think of anyone who had?'

'No. We certainly didn't. No, I can't.'

Sergeant Lawton appeared in the hall.

'Take Mrs Parry home now, Sergeant. Thank you, madam. I'm sorry it's been such a gruelling day.'

★ ★ ★

From the window he watched them get into the car and drive away, then, cursing, set about clearing up the shattered glass around his feet. Thus occupied, his attention returned once more to the sculpture. Detective-Inspector Walter lowered himself on to the window-seat and concentrated on assembling the information that he had so far gathered.

# 19

George, Alistair and Frances were called upon to give brief evidence at the inquest and the Coroner pronounced the cause of death as murder by person or persons unknown. Bernard's body was released for burial and once more the cast assembled, this time at the crematorium — Amelia and her husband, Frances, Liz and George, and Duncan granted a special day release to attend the funeral of his friend. Frances, standing next to him in the front pew, watched the coffin travel the brass rails towards the opened portcullis in the wall and willed herself to see through the wood for a last glimpse of her lover lying inside. It might have been an empty box, as empty and cold as her heart. Amelia was crying and Duncan's eyes were wet. Alistair stood like a ramrod, the epitome of controlled British grief, and none of the words seemed to have any relevance to Bernard. He had been his own religion, a law unto himself, but there wasn't apparently any civilized method of disposing of a body without benefit of clergy.

★ ★ ★

Duncan was unreceptive to her proffered comfort. His manner towards her was sullen and unforthcoming and after the service, back at the ritual bunfight which had been prepared by Dolly in their absence, Frances asked him if he still blamed her over the money. She was completely thunderstruck when he said, 'I've been thinking about that, Fran. I've only got your word for it that you lent Bernard that cash. You didn't by any chance appropriate it for your own business? It seems to me Liz and you have done phenomenally well in a short time.'

'If I had done that, I should have told you,' she said icily.

'Would you?'

'For Christ's sake, Duncan, there's no hope for either of us if you're going to be paranoid. You're coming home in less than two weeks now. We've got to make a go of things — more than ever. That means both forgiving and forgetting. We've both made mistakes.'

It had been impossible to discuss anything in depth then, and later he had had to go back to Sussex. Frances, strained by the daily dread of further investigations by the police, bruised by the loss of Bernard, and worried

289

sick at the prospect of the demands shortly to be put upon her by resumed connubiality, could only stagger forward from day to day with no clear picture of what would emerge at the end of the tunnel. Only her faith in her work and herself had not been eroded. The loss of the money was relatively unimportant in terms of security, because she knew herself capable of making more — enough for their needs. Only in that it would have represented her freedom from Duncan, she regretted it. Sometimes she wondered if she would have ever brought herself to leave him. Everything was changed, muddled and muddied. Nothing had been as it had seemed. Her priority was their survival — hers and Alistair's and Duncan's. Once again she sought refuge in positive activity.

'Thank heavens we can hang on to No. 6 until a couple of months after Duncan comes home,' she said to Liz. 'After that, God knows what will happen. I'll have to try to find a flat or something.'

She'd given Dolly and Liz the same story about the loan. Dolly had declaimed her as an arrant fool, whereas Liz had accepted the tale with an old-fashioned look which attested her cynicism, but had said nothing. It was Liz's unvoiced opinion that there was more in the violent mode of Bernard's death than met the eye and he had received his come-uppance as the result of some shady dealing. 'Somehow one couldn't imagine Bernard dying of old age, peacefully in bed,' she had said once to Frances, who had been able to smile.

'You can always move in with Kate and me. I felt guilty swanning about in that huge flat after it was extended. It could take three and a half people in it easily.'

Frances pressed her hand gratefully. 'Thanks, Liz, but I wouldn't hear of it. There's not just me to consider. There's Duncan as well.'

'Yes.' Liz looked narrowly at her friend. 'What are you going to do about him, Fran?'

'It's not up to me. He must do something about himself.'

'But will he? And if he doesn't, won't you?'

Frances laughed. 'I expect so. That's what he dreads. He's always throwing it at me. Honestly, Liz, I doubt if we have any points of contact any more.'

'Why bother, then?'

Frances remembered Bernard asking nearly the same question. 'Pride, I guess. Because I feel guilty too. Two reasons.' She shelved the problem of Duncan and gave all her attention to the trade figures in the European market into which they were on the point of breaking.

★ ★ ★

Alistair had had no subsequent visitation from the Inspector or his henchman. Apparently his alibi had been accepted as had Frances's on Dolly's corroboration. The Monday after the murder the papers had carried columns but mercifully no pictures, and for a day or two there had been a line to the effect that enquiries were proceeding — then nothing. Everyone had gone about their normal business. 'In the midst of life,' Frances thought. It reduced all the sound and fury of their little lives to insignificance.

★ ★ ★

Coming home from the shop a few days before Duncan's release, the unwelcome sight of Inspector Walter's car sitting in her small drive caused a small frisson of fear to tingle on the nape of Frances's neck. Concealing her apprehension, she managed to welcome him with a smile and invite him into the house. Before she had left that morning she had unearthed a couple of the trunks containing Duncan's clothes and his other effects from the front room, and these stood cluttering the hall and impeding progress. Frances explained their presence as she and Walter picked their way around them on their way to the sitting-room.

'My husband is coming home on Friday. I'm getting things prepared. Now, Inspector, what can I do for you? How are things going? Have you got any news?' She sat forward on her chair, all interest.

Inspector Walter was glad to see how much better she looked than she had when they had last met. She'd been through a tough time. He'd acquainted himself with the facts of her husband's case and admired the way she'd stuck by him. From all accounts she was a fighter. A woman of character. The higher the position, the more degrading the fall, and she'd apparently coped with the change in her circumstances better than most. Now she'd had to contend with sudden death and a substantial loss of capital. Yet she could smile. He smiled back, revealing the sharply pointed teeth of the carnivore.

'We are still checking, of course, but it appears that some of our original deductions were correct. For instance, we accept that the murderer came and went by the french windows, as it originally seemed. We now believe that his purpose was to kill Mr

King — not burglary, as he made it appear.'

Frances's heart, which had lifted at the good news contained in the first part of his explanation, sank leadenly at his rider.

'Why should anyone want to kill Mr King?'

'That, madam, has been the difficult one. You were right when you said he kept himself to himself. With your help we have been able to trace the few friends he appears to have had, and eliminated them. Your husband was closest to him. We know that it would have been impossible for him to have committed the crime. The same goes for yourself. Your sister supports your alibi, so does another tenant of her block of flats who testified she saw your car arrive just before eight o'clock that night. Sir Alistair and Lady Parry have two hundred and fifty witnesses to vouch for the fact that they were at the Trafalgar rooms at the time of the crime. Mr Bruton too was involved in a social gathering on Saturday evening. From a perusal of Bruton and King's books there would seem to be no reason why any of Mr King's clients should have a motive.'

Relief resurfaced. The all-important time of the murder had been undoubted, indelibly fixed. It was obviously not suspected that the assassin had ventured further than the one room.

'That eliminates just about everyone, Inspector. What grounds have you for persisting in the belief that it was not an act on the spur of the moment attendant upon a robbery?'

'Two factors, Mrs Parry, for both of which I am indebted to you. The money that Mr King borrowed from you and the fact that he had homosexual tendencies.'

It was going even better than she had dreamed. He seemed to have swallowed all the bait on the hook.

'His need for that money worried me — a man in his circumstances. It had to be something private — secret. One's mind naturally runs to women — an intrigue turned embarrassing — or, after what you told me, to men. Those kinds of liaison too often provide fodder for the blackmailer. There are degrees of insecurity, jealousies, undercurrents running higher than in average heterosexual relationships.'

'You suspect that Mr King was being blackmailed because he was a homosexual?'

Walter pursed his mouth. 'Either that or he was paying highly for his pleasure. I incline to the latter theory.'

'I see,' said Frances. She nearly laughed

out loud. She thought of Bernard's body as it had delighted and enthralled her, insatiably exulting in her womanhood, and defied Detective-Inspector Walter to search the world over for the man who could have interested Bernard sexually. They were safe home and dry. She was hardly listening to what he said next.

'And if I hadn't broken that wretched sculpture, who can say how long our enquiries might have taken?'

She looked at him woodenly, not understanding. 'I don't follow. What's the sculpture got to do with it?'

'I felt badly about breaking it. Sheer carelessness. You said it was valuable. I thought I'd better try to get it mended. I remembered you'd said it had been made by someone in the Bayswater Road. As a matter of fact his name was on a plaque under its base, did you know that?'

Frances shook her head dumbly. No, she hadn't known.

'Well, I sat and thought about it — collected all the pieces, and then some sixth sense reminded me of your exact words — 'an artistic protégé of Mr King's'. We policemen learn not to despise our hunches, Mrs Parry. I went along to see the young man in question. We had a conversation. It was very interesting. He's a self-confessed queer. One of these Gay libbers and proud of it. Yes, he knew Mr King pretty well — and the apartment, though he denied that their relationship was intimate, of course. He also admitted receiving sums of money from Mr King.' Inspector Walter licked his lips. He was getting into his stride. 'To complete the picture, he owns a Luger and he has no alibi for Saturday night.' Having arrived triumphantly at his conclusion, he sat back and awaited her applause.

Frances was appalled. Her face was frozen in shock, incredulity and uncertainty. 'But you can't convict on circumstantial evidence alone, surely, Inspector.'

'Depends on how many circumstances and I'd say from experience that there are too many here to let him off the hook.'

'But the sums of money could be accounted for by purchases. Mr King told me he bought what he could afford from time to time.'

'If they were, where are the items he purchased? They weren't in his flat. You must admit the sculpture stuck out like a sore thumb in those surroundings.'

'I know he was always buying and selling items,' Frances said weakly.

'Of course we'll check on it but apart from anything else he's a grisly little bit of work, this Jasper Banks. Mr King wasn't the only one in his clutches.'

'Is that his name?' Frances felt faint. 'I didn't know it.'

'You'll be hearing more of it, I don't wonder. Well, Mrs Parry, I must be leaving. Just came to tell you.' He rose and patted his jacket pockets complacently with the air of one having executed a job well done.

Frances stared at the door long after she had shut it behind him. She'd been too clever by half. 'You're so sharp you'll cut yourself one day,' her mother had been fond of saying. Well, she'd well and truly cut herself now. Of all the ill-starred coincidental bits of luck that Jasper Banks should be a fag who had nowhere to go on a Saturday night! They *had* to wait and ride it out. It wasn't possible that the police would keep him if they couldn't prove conclusively that he had done it, but what if, as Walter had said, he had had the means, opportunity and motive? Being innocent wouldn't save him. Suppose it came to a trial — to a sentence? No good supposing, except — supposing it was the ferret's way of flushing out the rabbit? On examination it seemed unlikely. If it had been a yarn to smoke them out, that meant the Inspector already suspected them. But there was no way in which he could. Their alibis were irrefutable — when he had said so Frances could have sworn he wasn't lying. She wondered whether she should ring Alistair, then decided against it. They'd kept their heads so far. Let him have the benefit of another good night's sleep.

★ ★ ★

Alistair read the four-line news item while he was eating his breakfast. Amelia breakfasted in bed, so he was alone and able to read it three times, then sit and stare into space, his toast and coffee forgotten, without comments being made upon his behaviour. He was feeling tired and unwell. 'A man is helping the police in their enquiries.' Nine times out of ten a euphemism for arrest. What man? Why didn't the press, usually vainglorious of their snooping scoops, say more? It was half past eight. If he rang Frances he might catch her before she left for work. The temptation to call her daily hung heavily upon him as it was. He had tried to resist it but he needed the comfort of her confidence that things were going according to plan and down at Falconers he felt cut off, although it was ridiculous to assume that by being nearer London he would have known any more. Frances had her work and Duncan's homecoming to plan for. At least Alistair's action had prevented their final break-up. Her days were occupied, taking her mind off what had happened for hours at a stretch, whereas his were empty and long. Sleep eluded him and he spent too many tedious nights restlessly searching the past, probing the future, trying to find a formula for enduring the present. It was Frances, not Bernard, who had murdered his sleep. He kept seeing the way she had looked at him out there in the garden when he had admitted that to save his skin he couldn't let her off the hook. She had pitied and despised him in that moment. He despised himself — but, Jesus Christ! — he hadn't expected her to be dragged in at all.

Alistair got up from the table and went into his study. Frances's voice was guarded as she answered the phone.

'Oh, it's you,' she said. 'I was going to ring you.'

'Have you seen the piece in the *Telegraph*?' he asked without preamble. 'It says a man is helping the police.'

'I did know. Inspector Walter told me last night.' Frances tried to keep her voice merely conversational. She hoped that Alistair would remember that the phone might be tapped.

'Last night? What did he say? Who is this man?'

'He's an artist. Jasper Banks. Bernard's friend who made the sculpture.'

'How in God's name did they get around to him?' The question came on a rising note of hysteria.

'Apparently he has all the qualifications. He's a homosexual, he's received sums of money from Bernard, he owns an automatic revolver and he has no alibi for Saturday night. They think Bernard was paying for his services, although he denies any such thing.'

'Services?'

'Homosexual. Jesus, he wasn't servicing the Hoover!'

'My God!' So she'd used that angle after all and been hoist with it. 'Will they charge him?'

'The Inspector said the evidence was pretty damning.'

There was a dumb silence at his end of the phone. He couldn't think of any safe way to phrase his fearful questions. Frances was equally helpless. She said tritely, 'We'll have to wait and see what happens.' It was a warning.

'Frances — '

'Don't worry. I'll keep you in the picture.'

'But — '

'I must go now. I'll be late for work. My love to you both.'

He was slow in replying, then he finally said, 'My love to you, Frances.'

He sat looking at the phone, feeling a great deal worse after so unsatisfactory an exchange. He realized she couldn't have said much more over the phone but she had sounded impatient and irritable. Of course she must be as worried as he was, but it was all very well to say they must wait and see. A man was being arrested and charged for his — Alistair's — crime. There was an outside chance the case might be thrown out before getting to trial, but if it weren't and he had sat tight until then before coming forward, how much worse would he make things for himself, in the long run? There would be the strain of weeks and months of uncertainty and indecision and at the end of it, doubly damnable disgrace. The stress wouldn't be his alone. Frances too would be under the sort of pressure he had no right to expect her to bear. It was criminal of him to have implicated her in the first place. He was back to square one and he needed a drink.

There was whisky in the tantalus on the chest and he poured himself a liberal shot and downed it. The spirit burned his gullet and hit his empty stomach like a bursting meteor. Frances had borne the brunt of all the Inspector's examinations. She would never voluntarily betray him, but if a day came when, for any reason, they finally broke her down, as what sort of a heel would he come out of it? The answer was of course that he wouldn't be coming out of anything — but going in. How many years did one get for premeditated murder? There would hardly be any extenuating circumstances to plead, not at that distance of time. From that point of view, better to give himself up now. The pit of his stomach, temporarily warmed by the whisky, chilled as the muscles there tightened. He sent another shot down to anaesthetize his fear, but regurgitated it on a wave of nausea and had to swallow it back, mingled with bile. He could well imagine the sensation it would cause, the publicity of his arrest coinciding with Duncan's release, all the circumstances of his son's case rehashed and resurrected publicly just at the time when he would be making a new start. He was lying to himself again. It wasn't Duncan for whom he feared the publicity. It was himself. He was tired, spent with fatigue and anxiety. His one burst of courage in eliminating Bernard had been a foolish old man's last-gasp attempt to revive his former glory. What price courage now? And there was Amelia. If she had found visiting Duncan humiliating, how would she feel about supporting a long-term prisoner? The answer was that she most likely wouldn't. He would lose her irrevocably, and without her, at the end of it all, what would be left? Amelia — Frances — Duncan — Jasper Banks — the names wove alcoholically into a nightmare sequence as his judgement vacillated at each new twist in his mental debate.

Shakily, he got to his feet and, taking a key from his watch-chain, moved to the wall safe above the gun cases and inserted the key. He had awoken with a headache which hadn't been helped by the whisky on an empty stomach, and a pulse throbbed in his temples with an increasingly painful persistence. In spite of it, he remembered the combination. Three numbers — his age, followed by Amelia's in the year the safe had been installed — thirty-six and thirty-two — they had been young and in love with each other and Falconers. He turned the key anti-clockwise for the third number. Seventy-nine, the number of his regiment in the war. The combination clicked and the door swung open revealing the contents of the chamber within. A jewel box of Amelia's, a copy of Alistair's will, and a manila envelope for which he reached and removed. With it in his hand he felt better, and clutching it he shuffled back to his desk. There seemed to be a weight attached to his left leg and he had trouble bringing it along after the right one. Ball and chain! He smiled grimly, thinking of manacled convicts — and of Amelia. The letter was his talisman. He was glad he had written it when he had, straight after Bernard's death. If he hadn't the courage in life, he had thought at least in death to be still capable of honour. However, in the light of recent events and Jasper Banks, he couldn't wait for death and might have to post it today. Alistair gazed upon the black typed words on the envelope. PRIVATE. FOR THE ATTENTION OF INSPECTOR WALTER. They were raised in a bump over the concealed shape of the cartridge case which he had failed to dispose of. Something had prevented him covering his tracks quite completely. Somewhere there had to be a record of what had happened, exonerating Frances — just in case. The letter represented a remnant of self-respect. It had taken him a long time to write it.

Alistair frowned as he grappled with the problem of what to do next. He'd got it out of the safe for some specific reason but this blinding head of his prevented him from thinking clearly. His mind directed his left hand to smooth and ease his aching brow, but he was surprised to look down and see that his arm had not obeyed the message. He tried again, but the obstinate member remained hanging uselessly down over the chair arm. There was a rushing sound like the arrival of a shell before it bursts and he was transported back to Cassino and tried to duck his head. After the explosion everything was very quiet and peaceful.

★ ★ ★

Amelia, coming to see why he had left his breakfast, found him unconscious in his chair, the left side of his face grotesquely palsied, and breathing with the stertorous respiration of advanced coma. His good wrist and hand lay across the letter protectively, obscuring the writing. In the shock of discovering him thus Amelia overlooked its significance. If she hadn't, doubtless she would have opened and examined its contents, but as it was, when Alistair had been carried upstairs, there were by then others present, and the letter was collared by the local constable who made it his business to see that it reached its designated destination.

# 20

'This letter is dated the day after Mr King's death, Mrs Parry. Sir Alistair evidently wrote it and lodged it in his safe against just such an eventuality as occurred — an innocent person being convicted of his crime either before or after his own death. No doubt he thought it unlikely, because I have to admit he had very ingeniously covered his own tracks, but that's what makes police work so fascinating, the psychology involved.'

'Psychology?' Frances asked weakly.

Detective-Inspector Walter had brought the news of Alistair's death to her at the office at the shop at three o'clock in the afternoon. He had died at midday without regaining consciousness, and coming so swiftly after her conversation with him earlier in the day, the news piled horror upon horror. Frances, hysterically feeling as if she were acting out a Greek drama with at least half as many corpses on her hands as in the last act of *Hamlet*, not knowing whether the existence of the letter left her on foot or on horseback as far as the law was concerned, could only tread warily and say as little as possible until

Walter clarified her position. She waited for his answer, wondering if he were referring to his own psycho-analysis of herself.

'Yes.' He seemed happy to elucidate. 'Another man would never have incriminated himself by leaving in evidence such a letter. He wouldn't have given a damn if we had suspected an innocent party. This man was one of the old school, though. Although he was capable of murdering Mr King, Sir Alistair couldn't have countenanced a chance of that happening. An interesting dichotomy, wouldn't you say?'

Frances said quietly, 'And Brutus is an honourable man!'

He looked at her, she thought, kindly. 'And so he was. You'll want to remember him that way. Weak, perhaps, but honourable. The murder was a kind of rough justice.'

She was surprised, but relieved. Surely he wouldn't be talking to her in this way if he had any suspicion of her? His tone was plainly consoling. She said, 'That doesn't sound like a policeman. Surely for you there's black and there's white?'

He looked at her chalk-white face stained with dried tears and not for the first time she stirred his admiration. The old man's death had been a body blow — not only his death but the revelation of what he had done. Walter had been aware of the closeness of the bond between them.

Frances, sensing his sympathy, chanced her arm. 'I suppose I couldn't see that letter, could I, Inspector, or you could read it to me?'

He didn't see why not. It wasn't a suicide note. Sir Alistair had died of natural causes. His death didn't hinge upon the murder and with any luck the letter itself need not be publicized in court and press as evidence. It would be good if he could spare this courageous woman that extra notoriety. What Parry had written could remain confidential to the police, Jasper Banks would be released and the file on Bernard King closed. He put the handwritten pages down in front of her and turned away to scrutinize the wild life wall calendar while she read.

★ ★ ★

The confession was written on Falconers notepaper, stamped at the top with the address and the Parry crest. It was not addressed to anyone particular, but was dated and went straight to the point.

This is to state that I, Alistair Parry, of the above address, murdered Bernard

King of Brandon Court on the evening of Saturday, 11th November, 1978. My motive for doing so was that for many years the victim had been blackmailing me over a business indiscretion of which I had been guilty some years ago, and contrary to the opinion of the rest of my family, I knew Bernard King for a crook and a swindler. He had drained me for many years and the strain of that, coupled with the knowledge of the utter reliance placed in him by my son and daughter-in-law increased my hatred for him. My worst fears were realized when my daughter-in-law told me of a substantial loan of money she had made to him in the belief that he intended to repay it. The sum constituted my son's savings and means of rehabilitating himself in life after serving a prison sentence, and from what I knew of Bernard King I had grounded suspicions that he had swindled him out of it. As far as I was concerned, he had to be stopped and that was the end of his run.

I had thought it out carefully. I had to be in town on the night of Saturday, 11th November. My wife and I were staying at my club adjacent to Belgrave Square. Making the excuse of wanting to rehearse the speech I was to give later, I locked myself in my room and set the tape-recorder going. While my wife was at the hairdresser, I slipped out of the club's side entrance and went to Brandon Court where I forced entry into Mr King's apartment via the fire-escape just after seven o'clock. The room was in darkness, the door open with a light coming in from the hall. He was upstairs, the radio was playing and he didn't hear me at first. I had time to take my Smith and Wesson, which he had appropriated for himself, as he did any of my possessions that took his fancy, off the wall and load it with a packed bullet. He came into the room and I shot him before he had time to put on the light. I arranged the room to look as though there had been a burglary, cleaned and replaced the gun, then went upstairs to look for his keys. I found them in his suit pocket. I had seen the sculpture many times before and Mr King had told me about how it had once triggered off the alarm. I also knew how the alarm worked. I had thought about this and how it could give me an extended alibi. I put the sculpture on the window-seat, switched it on, set the downstairs alarm circuit, leaving the front door open, and ran upstairs to replace the keys. Then I came downstairs and went out of the apartment, closing the front door on the latch only. I hadn't the key to switch off the warning buzzer but I reckoned that wouldn't matter or be heard once the siren was ringing. The lift was at the third floor and I used the stairs and front door for my exit. I was back at the club just after seven twenty-five. I explained my wet raincoat by saying I had accidentally dropped it in the shower. For proof that I am telling the truth I enclose the cartridge case of the bullet that killed Bernard King. My wife will corroborate that the gun once belonged to me.

I swear this to be the truth.

Signed: ALISTAIR PARRY

Frances came to the end of the businesslike account, but did not raise her head. She had thought she had the monopoly on improvisation but she had underestimated Alistair's talented imagination. The piece about the keys was a masterly touch, and all the rest was true in a manner of speaking, except for the grounds for blackmail. The latter was insubstantial and wouldn't bear checking, but with Alistair dead and the *modus operandi* so clearly spelled out it

312

was unlikely anyone would probe his given motive. Her eyes filled with tears again. In her heart she had condemned him for using her but at the final count he had exonerated her and expiated in full. She wondered if he had known he was going to die and then reminded herself that this letter had been written nearly three weeks ago. From her bowed face a tear ran on to the text and smudged the ink of his signature. Frances dabbed it with her handkerchief and handed the papers back to Walter.

'Does all this have to be made public?' she asked him.

'Not necessarily.' He told her why. 'But of course his wife and son — '

'Has she seen this?'

'Yes.'

'It must have been very painful for her.'

'I don't think Lady Parry chooses to believe it,' he said.

'No. I don't suppose she does.' Amelia's preference would be for a denial of unpleasantness. 'But you accept it?'

He inclined his head. 'As I told you, we realized the Smith and Wesson could have been the weapon but all the time we were up against the time factor. The sculpture too. Until I took it along to Jasper Banks I admit I didn't realize that the whole

313

arrangement was mobile. Brinker described a weird lamp, Parsons a glass ornament. It had been switched off by the time he and I appeared on the scene. We were slow. The window-seat seemed an unhandy place for it and I should have realized that when you replaced it so naturally on that table, it was obviously where it lived.'

'I never thought,' Frances said. 'Everything was in such a mess in that room.' She went on more slowly. 'I still find it impossible to believe that Mr King was a blackmailer, or that he intended to swindle Duncan and me.' She remembered Duncan. 'Does my husband know about his father?'

'Lady Parry has been allowed to telephone him. I myself have spoken to the Governor. Which brings me to a piece of more pleasant news for you both.'

'Oh?' It would have to be good, she thought wryly, in any way to mitigate the loss of Alistair. 'I could do with some of that, Inspector.'

'You were to have collected your husband on Friday, I believe. On account of what has happened, he is being released today. He will be travelling up later this afternoon with Sergeant Lawton who's been sent down to fetch him.' Walter had the satisfaction of seeing that he had delivered a complete surprise and prepared himself for her delighted gratitude.

'Today?' She was aware that her amazement and confusion were evident in the one word, and to qualify this reaction of modified rapture she added two others with a forced enthusiasm. 'That's marvellous.'

'I am very pleased too.' Obviously under the impression he had conferred a prize on her, he prepared to leave. 'I'll be on my way, then. You'll be wanting to get home to be there when he arrives.'

'Yes. Yes, of course.' She looked about her helplessly, doubtful as to what she should do first.

'Goodbye then, Mrs Parry.' He held out his hand to her and shook it. 'Good luck.'

He was really going out of her life. It was all really over — the lies, the suspicion, the fear of discovery. 'Just a moment, Inspector. You said you'd try to keep my father-in-law's part in all this from the press.'

'I can't promise, but I'll see what I can do.'

'Thank you.'

Liz, who had been hovering outside, saw him go and came in to find Frances still standing in a state of stupor. She wore a worried frown and scanned Frances's face anxiously. 'Not more bad news?'

315

Frances said dully, 'Alistair's dead. He had a stroke this morning.'

'Oh no! Oh Fran, I'm so sorry.'

'I'm sorry too. I was very fond of him.'

'I know you were. Had he been under the weather? I suppose it was all this worry over Bernard, and Duncan as well.'

'They couldn't have helped. They both played their part.' They were silent, each thinking her own thoughts.

'Liz, Duncan's coming home. Today. They've let him go early because of his father. A policeman's bringing him back. I must go home and prepare for him.' Still she made no effort to move.

Liz, uncertain whether to welcome this under the category of good or bad news, pressed her lips together.

Frances said, 'I don't know how to cope with him, Liz. It's too soon. I want more time.'

'You always knew he was coming at the end of the week,' Liz reminded her gently. 'You've had too much time apart already — that's the trouble.'

Frances sighed. She started collecting her things. 'No, that's not the trouble, Liz.' She shot her friend a wan smile. One day in the future she might or might not tell her the whole story, but first there was a more important challenge to be faced. Life seemed to be composed of one after the other with very little breathing space between. At least she'd know she would be satisfying Alistair's dearest wish, sticking with Duncan and striving to regain their past compatibility — she wasn't calling it happiness. Alistair hadn't said he'd acted as he had to prevent Bernard getting her, but Frances felt sure the desire must have formed an integral part of his motive.

'I'm afraid all my traumas have been very disruptive to my work. I promise you, Liz, with Duncan back and life reverting to normal, I shall be pulling my weight again. I'll have to leave you now, though.'

Liz put her hand on her arm and pressed it. 'Don't come in for the rest of the week. You'll both have some rehabilitating to do. Ring me. In the meantime, I'm so very sorry about Alistair, Fran. Take care.'

★ ★ ★

She hadn't got a fatted calf, and even if she had, it would have been in the freezer like everything else that it was too late to thaw for the return of the prodigal. On her way home Frances collected a couple of trout. She rushed back to No. 6 to prepare them

317

and the vegetables, lay the table for dinner *à deux*, and empty a chest of drawers for those clothes of Duncan's she had already sorted and whatever he would bring. Moving her pillows from the centre of the bed, she put two more for him on the left-hand side, trying to imagine herself lying face to face, body to body with him, a prospect that left her feeling as refrigerated as the fatted calf! Comforting herself with the thought that Duncan too would be bowed with shock and grief and that his spirits (and with luck much else!) would be flagging, she determined not to cross her bridges before she came to them. She had been the one to insist that it had to be a genuine effort on both sides, and if she didn't live up to that ideal, how could she expect him to? It was stupid of her not to have asked approximately what time she could expect him. She would have liked a bath, but was daunted by the likelihood of his arriving to find her nakedly at a disadvantage, and for the same reason she was unwilling to embark on any of a hundred waiting tasks. When the fire was lit and the house was ready, she fidgeted about, unable to concentrate on a book or the radio, ears pricked for the sound of a car. When it finally came, she ran into the hall, standing behind the closed front door, waiting for his ring before she opened it after a suitable pause. Tactfully Sergeant Lawton stood aside to allow them their reunion, but if either of them had expected Duncan to sweep her off her feet in a passionate embrace, both were doomed to disappointment.

'Hullo, Fran.' He looked gaunt and tired and he made no attempt to kiss her.

'Welcome home. Come along in.'

He went past her into the hall, hesitating on the threshold to throw back over his shoulder, 'Thank you, Sergeant.' It was a gesture of dismissal and a churlish one which Frances felt bound to moderate by an invitation to a drink. She was thankful when Lawton declined it. He and she exchanged a couple of pleasantries, then he got into the car and drove away and Frances followed Duncan slowly into the house.

It was somewhat disconcerting to find he had already made himself at home to the tune of appropriating the telephone for a call to his mother with whom he was engaged in conversation on Frances's entry. He didn't look up as she stood there, and presently she took herself into the kitchen, leaving the two of them to discuss funeral arrangements and who should be notified before the announcement of Alistair's death went into the papers. With the wind taken out of her sails, Frances leaned against the sink and waited until he had finished.

'Sorry about that,' he said, coming in to find her, 'but I promised to ring Mother when I could. She's been pretty good, organized the funeral for Tuesday and put all the necessary wheels in motion.' His voice was hard and matter-of-fact and she found him difficult to approach with the sympathy that she wanted to offer and had expected he would require.

'How is she?' she asked.

'As well as can be expected. The old medical jargon dies hard. It's as damnable for her as it is for me.' He was expresing anger, not grief. He laughed shortly. 'It's not easy to accept that your old man's a murderer.'

'Hadn't we better have a drink? Whisky?' She got it and he sat down at the kitchen table with the glass in his hand.

'It makes you laugh, doesn't it? My disgrace, my blot on the escutcheon! But I didn't murder anyone. When I think about all that crap about honour and duty I was dished, and how I never came up to scratch.' He jerked his head back emphatically to swallow.

In spite of her good intentions she said, 'Do you have to be so subjective? Can't you think of him a little?'

'I find it hard to.'

'So do I. He must have been very unhappy and pressed for a long time. I find that hard to think of.' She realized he'd only been in the house ten minutes and they were already arguing. In an attempt to mollify, she went on, 'With any luck none of his story is going to get out. Inspector Walter told me that his confession will be treated as confidential and as he died from natural causes there'll be no inquest. That's a lot to be thankful for.'

'I agree. It's more than I had.'

His sneer infuriated her but she must refuse to get rattled.

'You sound as if you want it all over the papers,' she said coldly.

'As far as I'm concerned they can print what they like. Nothing they write can do me any further harm.'

'Nor him,' she reminded him tartly. 'But there's your mother, and having been through it yourself, don't you want to spare his memory?'

'I don't owe either of them anything.' He said it bitterly, and she could see that he had conditioned himself to believe it. 'As for his memory, he killed my best friend. That's what I shall remember about him.'

'Your best friend was a blackmailer and a thief.'

'I don't necessarily believe either of those accusations, but even were they true — Bernard was still my best friend.'

'And wasn't your father still your father?' Her voice rose on impatience and irritation.

He chose to ignore the fact that she'd made a point. 'A man who sets himself up like Father shouldn't put himself in a position to be blackmailed. A 'business indiscretion'! That could cover an assortment of squalid little criminal deals as a result of which he eventually got himself knighted. As for the 'thief' part — there's nothing to prove Bernard didn't intend to repay the loan.'

She drew in her enraged breath for the luxury of shouting at him that there had never been any loan, but remembered in time that if she did so, she would then be asked her reason for saying that there had. It would have been immensely satisfying as well to have opened Duncan's eyes to the real motive for Bernard's blackmail, but it was safer to let sleeping dogs lie and to allow him to accept the story Alistair had been at pains to concoct and the one adopted by the police. Nothing in this world would change his attitude to his father. It didn't matter a jot to Alistair now and was solely Duncan's loss. Her anger expired and she shrugged her shoulders in resignation. 'I don't know why we're quarrelling about it. Nothing can change what's happened. I thought you'd be upset, that's all.'

He snorted righteously. 'I am, Fran, believe me I am. But not the way you expected. I feel badly let down.'

*He* felt let down! God above, that was rich! Her innate honesty rapidly cooled her indignation. He was more right than he knew. He had in all truth been let down, by herself as much as Bernard, and least of all by his father who was getting the blame. Misconstruing the look on her face, he added sarcastically, 'Now remind me that I let you down and that you stood by me.'

It wasn't worth answering. With artificial brightness she changed the subject. 'You haven't seen over the house yet.' In the context of his hostility the words sounded ridiculous.

He took in his surroundings with slight interest as if for the first time, then said abruptly, 'It doesn't matter. I shan't be staying.'

At first she thought he meant that he had to be with Amelia and she opened her mouth to say how of course she'd drive him down to Falconers in the morning, but he didn't mean that, as he proceeded to make clear.

'I'm not coming back to you, Fran.'

She stared at him and he stared back. She could see that uttering the words had taken an effort on his part, knocking some of the brusque assurance out of him.

She managed a word. 'Why?'

'I'm sorry, I can't take being pressed into the mould of your making. Trying to live up to you all over again. It will be worse now that you're successful in your own right and nothing will persuade me to come in under you and Liz. I'm sorry,' he repeated. 'I really don't want to hurt you.'

'But I don't want to force you to do anything. You can do what you like. I just want you to be happy.'

His smile was twisted. 'That's my Fran. Don't bawl me out. You're 'handling' me already.'

'That's unfair.'

'Probably, but that's how you make me feel.'

'Then I'm sorry too.'

There was an awkward pause, terminated by his apologetic cough. He said with more gentleness, 'I really think — I know it's better if I don't come back. I don't feel so badly about it since I know you've got your career and that whatever happens, Fran, you'll make out. As for the furniture and what's left of our money — well, surely we can reach an amicable arrangement between us. We're both adults.' He waited for a response.

She asked slowly, 'Do you mean you want a divorce?'

'Yes.' He was relieved to be over the hurdle.

'What will you do? Where will you go?'

'Oh, don't worry about me. Guy and I are going to buy the Basingstoke printers after all. I'll still put in whatever I can, but he's managed to find another backer to finance us.'

'Guy?' queried Frances stupidly.

'Guy Ainsley. Father told you about him.' His voice was enthusiastic now, on firmer ground. 'He's an incredible chap, Fran, with lots of vision and drive. I know we shall make a go of it.' His eyes were bright, even eager, and an absurd suspicion began to form in Frances's mind.

'What's he like?'

'Guy? Oh, tallish, athletic, a good bit younger than me, good-looking in a gangling sort of a way — amazing sense of humour. I've got a picture of him somewhere.' He struggled to get it out of his wallet. It was a colour photo of the two of them in prison shirts and trousers, their arms loosely hung across each other's shoulders. They were laughing, their heads inclined affectionately towards each other. He didn't look much more than a boy, a youth with attractively dark eyes and a weak mouth. Frances studied him and knew that he was the reason why Duncan was not coming home. He may have made her his excuse — God knew he had always needed one — but here was the root cause for his change of heart. Here was his next crutch, his latter-day David. She wondered how long it had been going on.

'I presume you're not in any hurry,' she said. 'We can wait two years and then do it in a civilized way. Unless of course there's anyone else you want to get married to sooner.' She held out the photograph and as he took it from her she met his eyes squarely. 'There won't be, will there?'

'No, I shan't be getting married again.' He had the grace to flush. 'I didn't realize — I shouldn't have done so in the first place.'

She wanted to laugh, aloud and long, when she thought of the pains Alistair had taken to protect his son's reputation, of her arrogant insistence that Duncan needed her, of her preparation for a self-sacrifice that was to be thrown back in her face, of the qualms she had experienced anticipating their physical reunion, and of the wasted trout. How amusing it all was. What a joke. How Bernard would have appreciated it with her. There was no pain in the loss of Duncan, only in brutal self-enlightenment. She would be free. She couldn't pretend it was a tragedy.

Duncan, unable to deduce her thoughts and feeling uncomfortable, tentatively suggested he rang for a taxi.

'Won't you stay for dinner?' The banality of the invitation provoked a fresh onset of mirth but she managed to keep a straight face suitable to the occasion.

'No, thank you, Fran. I'd better go.'

'You know where the phone is.'

'Thanks.'

He made the call and they stood awkwardly in the hall waiting for the taxi to arrive, like actors, word imperfect, awaiting the instructions of their prompter.

'I'll be in touch, of course.' He said it twice and she murmured that that would be fine. The car came at last and they both went eagerly to its summons. At the final moment he kissed her fleetingly upon both cheeks and she saw that he was not unmoved. She hadn't asked him where he was going. It seemed nothing any more to do with her, and when the sound of the taxi was out of hearing, she stepped back into

327

the house and closed the door. The sight of the table set for two in the sitting-room reminded her that she was famished. It was just as well Duncan hadn't stayed. She was hungry enough to polish off both fish.

## THE END

*Other titles in the*
*Ulverscroft Large Print Series:*

## THE GREENWAY
### Jane Adams

When Cassie and her twelve-year-old cousin Suzie had taken a short cut through an ancient Norfolk pathway, Suzie had simply vanished . . . Twenty years on, Cassie is still tormented by nightmares. She returns to Norfolk, determined to solve the mystery.

## FORTY YEARS
## ON THE WILD FRONTIER
### Carl Breihan & W. Montgomery

Noted Western historian Carl Breihan has culled from the handwritten diaries of John Montgomery, grandfather of co-author Wayne Montgomery, new facts about Wyatt Earp, Doc Holliday, Bat Masterson and other famous and infamous men and women who gained notoriety when the Western Frontier was opened up.

## TAKE NOW, PAY LATER
### Joanna Dessau

This fiction based on fact is the love-turning-to-hate story of Robert Carr, Earl of Somerset, and his wife, Frances.

## A TASTE FOR DEATH
### Peter O'Donnell
Modesty Blaise and Willie Garvin take on impossible odds in the shape of Simon Delicata, the man with a taste for death, and Swordmaster, Wenczel, in a terrifying duel. Finally, in the Sahara desert, the intrepid pair must summon every killing skill to survive.

## SEVEN DAYS FROM MIDNIGHT
### Rona Randall
In the Comet Theatre, London, seven people have good reason for wanting beautiful Maxine Culver out of the way. Each one has reason to fear her blackmail. But whose shadow is it that lurks in the wings, waiting to silence her once and for all?

## QUEEN OF THE ELEPHANTS
### Mark Shand
Mark Shand knows about the ways of elephants, but he is no match for the tiny Parbati Barua, the daughter of India's greatest expert on the Asian elephant, the late Prince of Gauripur, who taught her everything. Shand sought out Parbati to take part in a film about the plight of the wild herds today in north-east India.

## TO THE GARDEN ALONE
### Eve Ebbett

Widow Frances Morley's short, happy marriage was childless, and in a succession of borders she attempts to build a substitute relationship for the husband and family she does not have. Over all hovers the shadow of the man who terrorized her childhood.

## CONTRASTS
### Rowan Edwards

Julia had her life beautifully planned — she was building a thriving pottery business as well as sharing her home with her friend Pippa, and having fun owning a goat. But the goat's problems brought the new local vet, Sebastian Trent, into their lives.

## MY OLD MAN AND THE SEA
### David and Daniel Hays

Some fathers and sons go fishing together. David and Daniel Hays decided to sail a tiny boat seventeen thousand miles to the bottom of the world and back. Together, they weave a story of travel, adventure, and difficult, sometimes terrifying, sailing.

## McLEAN AT THE GOLDEN OWL
### George Goodchild

Inspector McLean has resigned from Scotland Yard's CID and has opened an office in Wimpole Street. With the help of his able assistant, Tiny, he solves many crimes, including those of kidnapping, murder and poisoning.

## KATE WEATHERBY
### Anne Goring

Derbyshire, 1849: The Hunter family are the arrogant, powerful masters of Clough Grange. Their feuds are sparked by a generation of guilt, despair and ill-fortune. But their passions are awakened by the arrival of nineteen-year-old Kate Weatherby.

## A VENETIAN RECKONING
### Donna Leon

When the body of a prominent international lawyer is found in the carriage of an intercity train, Commissario Guido Brunetti begins to dig deeper into the secret lives of the once great and good.

## DOUBLE INDEMNITY — MURDER FOR INSURANCE
### Jad Adams

This is a collection of true cases of murderers who insured their victims then killed them — or attempted to. Each tense, compelling account tells a story of cold-blooded plotting and elaborate deception.


## THE PEARLS OF COROMANDEL
### By Keron Bhattacharya

John Sugden, an ambitious young Oxford graduate, joins the Indian Civil Service in the early 1920s and goes to uphold the British Raj. But he falls in love with a young Hindu girl and finds his loyalties tragically divided.


## WHITE HARVEST
### Louis Charbonneau

Kathy McNeely, a marine biologist, sets out for Alaska to carry out important research. But when she stumbles upon an illegal ivory poaching operation that is threatening the world's walrus population, she soon realises that she will have to survive more than the harsh elements . . .

## THE DARKENING LEAF
### Caroline Stickland

On storm-tossed Chesil Bank in 1847, the young lovers, Philobeth and Frederick, prevent wreckers mutilating the apparent corpse of a young woman. Discovering she is still alive, Frederick takes her to his grandmother's home. But the rescue is to have violent and far-reaching effects . . .

## A WOMAN'S TOUCH
### Emma Stirling

When Fenn went to stay on her uncle's farm in Africa, the lovely Helena Starr seemed to resent her — especially when Dr Jason Kemp agreed to Fenn helping in his bush hospital. Though it seemed Jason saw Fenn as little more than a child, her feelings for him were those of a woman.

## A DEAD GIVEAWAY
### Various Authors

This book offers the perfect opportunity to sample the skills of five of the finest writers of crime fiction — Clare Curzon, Gillian Linscott, Peter Lovesey, Dorothy Simpson and Margaret Yorke.